A TRACE OF MURDER

(A KERI LOCKE MYSTERY—BOOK 2)

BLAKE PIERCE

D1157632

BOOKS BY BLAKE PIERCE

RILEY PAIGE MYSTERY SERIES
ONCE GONE (Book #1)
ONCE TAKEN (Book #2)
ONCE CRAVED (Book #3)
ONCE LURED (Book #4)
ONCE HUNTED (Book #5)
ONCE PINED (Book #6)
ONCE FORSAKEN (Book #7)
ONCE COLD (Book #8)

MACKENZIE WHITE MYSTERY SERIES
BEFORE HE KILLS (Book #1)
BEFORE HE SEES (Book #2)
BEFORE HE COVETS (Book #3)
BEFORE HE TAKES (Book #4)
BEFORE HE NEEDS (Book #5)

AVERY BLACK MYSTERY SERIES
CAUSE TO KILL (Book #1)
CAUSE TO RUN (Book #2)
CAUSE TO HIDE (Book #3)
CAUSE TO FEAR (Book #4)

KERI LOCKE MYSTERY SERIES
A TRACE OF DEATH (Book #1)
A TRACE OF MURDER (Book #2)
A TRACE OF VICE (Book #3)

CHAPTER ONE

The long hallway was dark. Even with her flashlight on, Keri had trouble seeing more than about ten feet in front of her. She ignored the pit of fear in her stomach and pressed on. With one hand holding the light and the other grasping her gun, she inched forward. Finally she made it to the basement door. Every part of her told her she'd finally found the place. This was where her little Evie was being held.

Keri pushed open the door and stepped onto the first creaky wooden step. The darkness here was even more overwhelming than in the hall. As she slowly made her way down the stairs, it occurred to her how odd it was to find a home with a basement in Southern California. This was the first one she'd ever encountered. Then she heard something.

It sounded like a child crying—a little girl, maybe eight. Keri called out to her and a voice called back.

"Mommy!"

"Don't worry, Evie, Mommy's here!" Keri shouted back as she hurried down the stairs. Even as she did, something was eating at her, telling her this wasn't quite right.

It wasn't until her toe snagged on a step and she lost her balance, falling forward into nothingness, that she realized what had been bothering her. Evie had been missing for five years. How could she still sound the same?

But it was too late to do anything about that now as she hurtled through the air toward the floor. She girded herself for the impact. But it didn't come. To her horror, she realized she was falling down a seemingly endless pit, the air getting colder, nonstop wailing all around her. She had failed her daughter once again.

Keri woke with a start, sitting bolt upright in her car. It took a moment for her to realize what was happening. She wasn't in an endless pit. She wasn't in a creepy basement. She was in her battered Toyota Prius in the police station parking lot, where she had fallen asleep while eating her lunch.

The cold she'd felt was from the open window. The wailing was actually the siren of a police car leaving the lot on a call. She was drenched in sweat and her heart was beating fast. But none of it was real. It was just another horrible, hope-crushing nightmare. Her daughter, Evelyn, was still missing.

1

Keri shook the cobwebs from her head, took a swig from her water bottle, got out, and headed back inside the station, reminding herself she was no longer just a mom: she was also a Missing Persons detective for the LAPD.

Her multiple injuries forced her to move gingerly. She was still only two weeks removed from her brutal encounter with a violent child abductor. Pachanga, at least, had gotten what he'd deserved after Keri rescued the senator's daughter. Thinking of it made the sharp pains she still felt all over her body more tolerable.

The doctors had only let her take off the soft-sided face protector a few days ago, after determining her fractured eye socket was healing well enough. Her arm was still in a sling from Pachanga breaking her collarbone. She'd been told she could remove it in another week but was considering dumping it early because it was so annoying. There was nothing to be done about her cracked ribs other than wear protective padding. That bothered her, too, as it made her look about ten pounds heavier than her usual 130 fighting weight. Keri wasn't a vain woman. But at thirty-five, she liked that she could still turn heads. With the pads bulging against her blouse at the waist and riding above her work slacks, she doubted she was doing much of that.

Because of the time off she'd been given to recover, her brown eyes weren't as bloodshot with exhaustion as usual and her dirty blonde hair, tied back in a simple ponytail, had actually been shampooed. But the fractured orbital bone had left the side of her face with a big yellow bruise which was only now starting to fade, and the sling didn't add to her appeal. This probably wasn't the ideal time to go on any first dates.

The thought of dating reminded her of Ray. Her partner for the last year and friend for six before that was still recovering in the hospital from having been shot in the stomach by Pachanga. Luckily, he was doing well enough that he'd recently been moved from the local hospital near the shooting to Cedars-Sinai Medical Center in Beverly Hills. That was only a twenty-minute drive from the station, so Keri could visit him often.

Yet at no point during those visits had either of them addressed the growing romantic tension she knew they were both feeling.

Keri took a deep breath before making the familiar but nerve-wracking walk through the station bullpen. It felt like her first day back. She could still feel eyes on her. Every time she walked past her co-workers, she sensed their furtive, darting looks and wondered what they were thinking.

2

Did they all still just consider her a rule-breaking loose cannon? Had she gotten any grudging respect for taking down a child-abducting killer? How long would being the only female detective in the squad make her feel like a permanent outsider?

As she walked past them all in the hustle and bustle of the station and eased herself into her desk chair, Keri tried to control the pit of resentment rising in her chest and just focus on the work. At least the place was packed and as chaotic as ever, and in that reassuring way, nothing had changed. The station was crowded with civilians filing complaints, perps being booked, and detectives on the phones, following up on leads.

Keri had been limited to desk duty since her return. And her desk was full. Ever since she got back, she'd been awash in a sea of paperwork. There were dozens of arrest reports to review, search warrants to procure, witness statements to evaluate, and evidence reports to examine.

She suspected that because she wasn't allowed to go out on cases yet, all her colleagues were pushing their busy work on her. Luckily, she was supposed to be allowed to return to the field tomorrow. And the secret truth was that she didn't mind being office-bound for one reason: Pachanga's files.

When the cops searched his house after the incident, they'd found a laptop. Keri and Detective Kevin Edgerton, the precinct's resident tech guru, had cracked Pachanga's password, managing to open his files. Her hope was that the files would lead to discovery of multiple missing children, maybe even her own daughter.

Unfortunately, what had seemed at first like the mother lode of information on multiple abductions had proven difficult to access. Edgerton had explained that the encrypted files could only be opened with the proper code-breaking cipher, which they didn't have. Keri had spent the last week learning everything she could about Pachanga in the hopes of cracking the code. But so far, she'd come up empty.

As she sat there reviewing files, Keri's thoughts returned to something that had been eating at her since she'd resumed work. When Pachanga kidnapped Senator Stafford Penn's daughter, Ashley, he'd done it at the behest of the senator's brother, Payton. The two men had been in communication on the dark web for months.

Keri couldn't help but wonder how a senator's brother had managed to get in touch with a professional abductor. It wasn't like they traveled in the same circles. But they did have one thing in common. Both men were represented by a lawyer named Jackson Cave.

Cave's office was high atop a downtown skyscraper, but many of his clients were far more earthbound. In addition to his corporate work, Cave had a long history of representing rapists, kidnappers, and pedophiles. If Keri was being generous, she suspected it was simply because he knew he could gouge such unpleasant clients. But part of her thought he actually got off on it. Either way, she despised him.

If Jackson Cave had put Payton Penn and Alan Pachanga in touch, it stood to reason that he also knew how to access all their encrypted files. Keri was sure that somewhere in that fancy high-rise office of his was the cipher she needed to break the code and discover details on all those missing children, maybe even her own. She resolved that one way or another, legally or not, she was getting into that office.

As she started to think how that might be accomplished, Keri noticed a twenty-something female uniformed officer walking slowly in her direction. She waved her over.

"What's your name again?" Keri asked, uncertain if she should already know.

"Officer Jamie Castillo," the young, dark-haired officer answered. "I only just got out of the academy. I was reassigned here the week you were in the hospital. I was originally at West LA Division."

"So I shouldn't feel too bad for not knowing who you are?"

"No, Detective Locke," Castillo said firmly.

Keri was impressed. The gal had confidence and a sharpness in her dark eyes that suggested keen intelligence. She also looked like she could take care of herself. Easily five foot eight, she had a sinewy, athletic frame that suggested tussling would be unwise.

"Good. What can I do for you?" Keri asked, trying not to sound intimidating. There weren't a lot of female cops in Pacific Division and Keri didn't want to scare any of them off.

"I've been covering the station's tip line for the last few weeks. As you might suspect, a ton of them were related to your run-in with Alan Pachanga and the statement you made afterward about trying to find your daughter."

Keri nodded, remembering. After she'd rescued Ashley, the department held a big press conference to celebrate the happy outcome.

Still in her wheelchair, Keri had praised Ashley and her family before co-opting the conference to mention Evie. She'd held up her picture and begged the public to offer any information that might help in her search. Her immediate supervisor, Lieutenant Cole Hillman, had been so pissed at her for using a department victory as a tool in her personal crusade that Keri thought he would have fired her on the spot if he could have. But since she was a wheelchair-bound, teenage-rescuing hero, he couldn't.

Even when she was stuck in the hospital, Keri had heard through the grapevine that he was annoyed when the department started getting inundated with hundreds of calls daily.

"I'm sorry you got stuck with that assignment," Keri said. "I guess I just wanted to make the most of the opportunity and didn't think about who would have to deal with the fallout. I assume all the calls were dead ends?"

Jamie Castillo hesitated, as if wondering whether she was making the right decision. Keri could see the wheels turning in the younger woman's head. She watched her calculating the right move and couldn't help but like her. It felt like she was watching a younger version of herself.

"Well," Castillo finally said, "most were easily dismissed as being from unstable people or simply pranks. But we got one call this morning that was somehow different. It had a straightforwardness that made me take it more seriously."

Almost immediately, Keri's mouth went dry and she felt her heart start to race.

Keep cool. It's probably nothing. Don't overreact.

"Can I hear it?" she asked more calmly than she'd thought possible.

"I've already forwarded it to you," Castillo said.

Keri looked at her phone and saw the blinking light indicating she had a voicemail. Trying not to look desperate, she slowly picked up the receiver and checked it.

The voice on the message was raspy, almost metallic sounding and hard to understand, made even more difficult by a banging noise in the background.

"I saw you on TV talking about your girl," it said. "I want to help. There's an abandoned warehouse in Palms, across from the Piedmont Generating Station. Check it out."

That was all there was to it—just a gravelly male voice offering a vague tip. So why were her fingertips tingling with adrenaline? Why was she having trouble swallowing? Why did her thoughts suddenly flash on potential images of what Evie might look like now?

5

Perhaps it was because the call had none of the earmarks of the standard hoax calls. It didn't try to draw attention to itself, which was what clearly got Castillo's attention. And that same element— its straightforward blandness—was the quality currently making beads of sweat trickle down Keri's back.

Castillo was watching her expectantly.

"You think it's legit?" she asked.

"Hard to tell," Keri answered evenly, despite her elevated heart rate, as she punched the generating station into Google Maps. "We'll check where the call originated from later and have tech try to scrub the message to see what else can be gleaned from the voice and background noise. But I doubt they'd be able to determine much. Whoever made this call was careful."

"That's what I thought too," Castillo agreed. "No name given, clear attempt to mask the voice, distracting noise in the background. It just felt...different from the others."

Keri was only half-listening as she looked at the map on her screen. The generating station was located on National Boulevard, just south of the 10 Freeway. Checking satellite imagery, she verified that there was a warehouse across the street. Whether it was abandoned, she didn't know.

But I'm about to find out.

She looked at Castillo and felt a rush of gratitude toward her— and also something she hadn't felt in a very long time for a fellow officer: admiration. She had a good feeling about her, and was glad she was here.

"Good work, Castillo," she said belatedly to the young officer, who was also staring at the screen. "So good that I think I better go check it out."

"You need company?" Castillo asked hopefully as Keri stood and gathered her things to head out for the warehouse.

But before she could answer, Hillman poked his head out of his office and yelled across the bullpen to her.

"Locke, I need you in my office now." He glared at her. "We've got a new case."

CHAPTER TWO

Keri stood frozen in place. She was consumed by a flood of conflicting emotions. Technically, this was good news. It looked like she was being put back on field duty a day early, a sign that Hillman, despite his issues with her, felt she was ready to resume her normal responsibilities. But part of her just wanted to ignore him and go straight to the warehouse this second.

"Today, please," Hillman called out, snapping her out of her momentary indecision.

"Coming, sir," she said. Then turning to Castillo with a little half-smile, she added, "To be continued."

When she stepped into Hillman's office, she noticed that his typically wrinkled brow was even more scrunched up than usual. Every one of his fifty years was visible on his face. His salt and pepper hair was mussed as usual. Keri could never tell if he didn't notice or just didn't care. He wore a jacket but his tie was loose and his ill-fitting shirt couldn't hide his slight paunch.

Sitting on the old, beat-up loveseat against the far wall was Detective Frank Brody. Brody was fifty-nine years old and less than six months from retirement. Everything about his demeanor reflected that, from his barely competent attempts at politeness to his disheveled, ketchup-stained dress shirt, nearly bursting at the buttons against his formidable girth, to his loafers, which were splitting at the seams and looked like they might fall apart at any moment.

Brody had never struck Keri as the most dedicated and hard-working of detectives, and recently he seemed more interested in his precious Cadillac than in solving cases. He usually worked Robbery-Homicide but had been reassigned to Missing Persons with the unit short-handed because of Keri's and Ray's injuries.

The move had put him in a permanently foul mood, which was only reinforced by disdain at potentially having to work with a woman. He was truly a man of a different generation. She'd actually once overheard him say, "I'd rather work with bricks and turds than chicks and birds." The feeling, though maybe stated in a slightly different way, was mutual.

Hillman motioned for Keri to sit in the metal folding chair across from his desk, then took the caller off mute and spoke.

"Dr. Burlingame, I'm here with the two detectives I'm going to be sending to meet with you. On the line are Detectives Frank Brody and Keri Locke. Detectives, I'm speaking to Dr. Jeremy

7

Burlingame. He's concerned about his wife, whom he hasn't been able to reach for more than twenty-four hours. Doctor, can you please repeat what you told me?"

Keri pulled out her notebook and pen to take notes. She was immediately suspicious. In any case of a missing wife, the first suspect was always the husband and she wanted to hear the timbre of his voice the first time he spoke.

"Of course," the doctor said. "I drove to San Diego yesterday morning to help perform a surgery. The last time I spoke to Kendra was before I left. I got home very late last night and ended up sleeping in a guest room so as not to wake her up. This morning I slept in since I didn't have any patients to see."

Keri wasn't sure if Hillman was recording the conversation so she scribbled furiously, trying to keep up as Dr. Burlingame continued.

"When I went into the bedroom, she was gone. The bed was made. I assumed she'd just left the house before I got up so I texted her. I didn't hear back—again, not that unusual. We live in Beverly Hills and my wife attends a lot of local charity functions and events and she typically silences her phone for them. Sometimes she forgets to turn the volume back on."

Keri wrote everything down, evaluating the veracity of each comment. So far nothing she'd heard sounded warning bells but that didn't mean much. Anyone could hold it together on the phone. She wanted to see his demeanor when confronted in person by LAPD detectives.

"I went to work and called her again on the way in—still no answer," he continued. "Around lunchtime I started to get worried. None of her friends had heard from her. I called our maid, Lupe, who said that she hadn't seen Kendra today or yesterday. That's when I really started to worry. So I called nine-one-one."

Frank Brody leaned in and Keri could tell he was going to interrupt. She wished he wouldn't but there was nothing she could do to stop him. She typically preferred to let an interviewee go on as much as they liked. Sometimes they got comfortable and made mistakes. But apparently Brody didn't share her philosophy.

"Dr. Burlingame, why didn't your call get routed to the Beverly Hills Police Department?" he asked. His gruff tone carried no sense of sympathy. It sounded to Keri like he was wondering how he'd gotten stuck with the case.

"I guess because I'm calling you from my office, which is in Marina del Rey. Does it really matter?" he asked. He sounded lost.

"No, of course not," Hillman assured him. "We're happy to help. And our missing persons unit would likely have been called in by BHPD anyway. Why don't you return to your house and my detectives will meet you there around one thirty. I have your home address."

"Okay," Burlingame said. "I'm leaving now."

After he hung up, Hillman looked at his two detectives.

"Initial thoughts?" he asked.

"She probably just ran off to Cabo with some of her girlfriends and forgot to tell him," Brody said without hesitation. "That or he killed her. After all, it's almost always the husband."

Hillman looked at Keri. She thought for a second before speaking. Something about applying the usual rules to this guy didn't feel right, but she couldn't put her finger on why.

"I'm tempted to agree," she finally said. "But I want to look this guy in the face before I draw any conclusions."

"Well, you're about to get your chance," Hillman said. "Frank, you can head out. I need to talk to Locke for a minute."

Brody gave her a malicious smile as he left, like she'd gotten detention and he'd somehow escaped it. Hillman closed the door behind him.

Keri braced herself, certain that whatever was coming couldn't be good.

"You can head out in a second," he said, his tone softer than she'd anticipated. "But I wanted to remind you of a few things before you go. First, I think you know I wasn't very happy about your stunt at the press conference. You put your own needs ahead of the department. You get that, right?"

Keri nodded.

"That said," he continued, "I'd like for us to get a fresh start. I know you were in a bad way at that moment and saw this as a chance to shine a light on your daughter's disappearance. I can respect that."

"Thank you, sir," Keri said, slightly relieved but suspicious that a hammer was yet to drop.

"Still," he added, "just because the press loves you doesn't mean I won't kick you out on your ass if you pull any of your typical lone wolf shit. Are we clear?"

"Yes, sir."

"Good. Lastly, please take it easy. You're less than a week out of the hospital. Don't do anything to put yourself back in there, okay? Dismissed."

Keri left his office, mildly surprised. She'd been expecting a dressing down. But she hadn't been prepared for the slight hint of concern for her well-being.

She looked around for Brody before realizing he must have already left. Apparently he didn't even want to share a car with a female detective. Normally she'd be annoyed but today it was a blessing in disguise.

As she headed for her car, she stifled a smile.

I'm back on field duty!

It wasn't until she'd been assigned a new case that she realized just how much she'd missed it. The familiar excitement and anticipation started to take hold and even the pain in her ribs seemed to dissipate slightly. The truth was that unless she was solving cases, Keri felt like a piece of her was missing.

She also couldn't help but grin about something else—she was already planning to violate two of Hillman's orders. She was about go lone wolf *and* not take it easy at the same time.

Because she was making a pit stop on her way to the doctor's house.

She was going to check out that abandoned warehouse.

CHAPTER THREE

With her siren on top of her battered Prius, Keri weaved in and out of traffic, her fingers gripped tight on the wheel, her adrenaline rising. The Palms warehouse was on the way to Beverly Hills, more or less. That was how Keri justified prioritizing the search for her daughter, missing five years ago last week, over the hunt for a woman who'd been gone less than a day.

But she had to get there quick. Brody had a head start in getting to Burlingame's house so she could get there after him. But if she showed up too much later, Brody was sure to rat her out to Hillman.

He'd use any excuse he could to avoid working with her. And telling the boss she'd delayed an investigation by arriving late to a witness interview was right up his alley. That left her only a few minutes to check out the warehouse.

She parked on the street and headed for the main gate. The warehouse was in between a self-storage place and a U-Haul rental outlet. The hum of the generating station across the street was disturbingly loud. Keri wondered if she was risking cancer just standing there.

The warehouse was surrounded by cheap fencing designed to keep vagrants and druggies out, but it wasn't hard for Keri to slide through the gap between the poorly locked gates. As she approached the front door of the complex, she noticed the sign for the place lying on the ground, covered in dust. It read *Priceless Item Preservation.*

There was nothing priceless inside the empty, cavernous warehouse. In fact, there was nothing inside at all other than a few turned over metal folding chairs and some mounds of crumbled drywall. The whole place had been cleared out. Keri walked the entire complex, looking for any clue that might relate to Evie, but couldn't find anything.

She knelt down, hoping that a different perspective might offer something fresh. Nothing jumped out at her, although there was something slightly odd at the far end of the warehouse. One metal folding chair was sitting upright with a pile of drywall debris resting on the seat, delicately balanced over a foot high. It seemed unlikely that it would have gotten that way without help.

Keri walked over and looked more closely. She felt like she was searching for connections where there were none. Still, she moved the chair aside, ignoring the drywall that teetered briefly before tumbling to the floor.

She was surprised by the sound when it hit the concrete. Instead of the expected thud, there was a hollow echo. Feeling her heart suddenly begin to beat faster, Keri kicked the debris away and stomped on the spot where it had fallen—another hollow echoing sound. She ran her hand along the floor and discovered that the spot that had been under the metal folding chair was not actually concrete but wood painted gray to blend in with the rest of the flooring.

Trying to control her breathing, she searched the wooden piece with her fingers until she felt a small raised bump. She pushed in on it, heard the sound of a latch opening, and felt one end of the wood piece pop up. She reached under and pulled the square chunk of wood, about the size of a manhole cover, from its grooved slot.

Below it was a space about ten inches deep. There was nothing inside. No papers, no equipment. It was too small to hold a person. At most, it could maybe have housed a small safe.

Keri felt around the edges for another hidden button but found nothing else. She wasn't sure what could have been here before but it was gone now. She sat down on the hard concrete next to the hole, not sure what to do next.

She looked at her watch. It was 1:15. She was supposed to be in Beverly Hills in fifteen minutes. Even if she left now, it would still be close. Frustrated and annoyed, she quickly put the wooden cover back in place, slid the chair back where it had been, and left the building, glancing at the sign on the ground once more.

Priceless Item Preservation. Is the name of the business some kind of clue or am I just being punked by some cruel asshole? Is someone telling me what I have to do to preserve Evie, my most precious item?

The last thought sent a wave of anxiety through Keri. She felt her knees buckle and dropped to the ground awkwardly, trying to prevent any further damage to her left arm, which was nestled uselessly in the sling across her chest. She used her right hand to stop herself from completely collapsing.

Bent over, with a cloud of dust rising around her, Keri closed her eyes tight and tried to force away the dark thoughts closing in on her. A brief vision of her little Evie forced itself into her brain.

She was still eight in the vision, her blonde pigtails bouncing on her head, her face white with terror. She was being tossed inside a white van by a blond man with a tattoo on the right side of his neck. Keri heard the thud as her tiny body slammed against the wall of the van. She saw the blond man stab a teenage boy who tried to stop him. She saw the van pull out and tear off down the road, leaving her far behind as she chased after it with bloodied, bare feet.

It was all still so vivid. Keri choked back tears as she pushed the memory away, trying to force herself back into the present. After a few moments she got control again. She took a few long, slow breaths. Her vision cleared and she felt strong enough to push herself upright.

This was the first flashback she'd had in weeks, since before the confrontation with Pachanga. Part of her had hoped they were gone for good—no such luck.

She felt the ache in her collarbone from the jarring when she'd reached out to brace herself as she fell. In frustration, she pulled off the sling. It was more of a hindrance than a help at this point. Besides, she didn't want to look weak in any way when she met with Dr. Burlingame.

The interview with Burlingame—I've got to go!

She managed to stumble back to her car and pull out into traffic, this time without the siren. She needed quiet for the call she was about to make.

CHAPTER FOUR

Keri felt a nervous pit in her stomach as she punched in the number of Ray's hospital room and waited while it rang. Officially, there was no reason for her to feel nervous. After all, Ray Sands was her friend and her partner in the Missing Persons Unit of LAPD's Pacific Division.

As the phone continued to ring, her mind drifted back to the time before they were partners, when she was a professor of criminology at Loyola Marymount University and served as a consultant for the department, helping him out on a few cases. They had hit it off immediately and he'd returned the professional favor by occasionally speaking to her classes.

After Evelyn was taken, Keri tumbled down a black hole of despair. Her marriage fell apart, and she took to drinking heavily and sleeping with multiple students at the university. Eventually she was fired.

It was soon thereafter, when she was nearly broke, drunk, and living on a decrepit old houseboat in the marina that he came by again. He convinced her to enroll in the police academy as he had done when his life had fallen apart. Ray had offered her a lifeline, a way to reconnect with the world and find meaning in her life. She took it.

After graduating and serving as a uniformed officer, she was promoted to detective, and she asked to be assigned to Pacific Division, which covered much of West Los Angeles. It was where she lived and the area she knew best. It was also Ray's division. He requested her as a partner and they'd been working together for a year when the Pachanga case put them both in the hospital.

But it wasn't the status of Ray's recovery that had Keri feeling nervous. It was the status of their relationship. Something more than friendship had developed in the last year, as they worked so closely together. They both felt it but neither was willing to acknowledge it out loud. Keri felt pangs of jealousy when she called Ray's apartment and a woman answered. He was a notorious and unrepentant ladies' man so it shouldn't have come as a surprise to her, but the feeling of envy was still there, despite her best efforts.

And she knew he felt the same way. She'd seen his eyes flash when they were on a case and a witness came on to her. She could almost feel him tense up beside her.

Even with him so close to death after getting shot, neither of them had been willing to address the issue. Part of Keri thought it was inappropriate to focus on such trivialities when he was recovering from life-threatening injuries. But another part of her was simply terrified of what would happen if things were out in the open.

So they both ignored it. And because neither was used to hiding things from the other, it had gotten awkward. As Keri listened to the ringing phone in Ray's hospital room, she half hoped he'd pick up and half hoped he wouldn't. She needed to talk to him about the anonymous call and what she'd discovered at the warehouse. But she didn't know how to start the conversation.

It ended up not mattering. After ten rings, she hung up. There was no voicemail on the hospital phone, which meant Ray likely wasn't in bed. She decided not to try his cell. He was probably in the bathroom or at a physical therapy session. She knew he'd been itching to get moving again and had finally gotten the go-ahead to start two days ago. Ray was a former professional boxer and Keri was certain he'd spend every available moment working to get back in fighting, or at least working, shape.

Unable to bounce her thoughts off her partner, Keri tried to force the warehouse trip out of her head and focus on the case at hand—missing person Kendra Burlingame.

With one eye on the road and the other on her phone's GPS, Keri quickly wound her way through the twisty Beverly Hills streets up into the secluded part of the community above the city. The higher into the hills she got, the more winding the roads were and the further back the homes got from the street. Along the way, she reviewed what she knew about the case so far. It wasn't much.

Jeremy Burlingame, despite his profession and where he lived, liked to keep a low profile. It took some quick digging by co-workers back at the station to learn the forty-one-year-old was a renowned plastic surgeon known both for doing cosmetic work on celebrities and for offering pro-bono surgery to children with facial deformities.

Kendra Burlingame, thirty-eight, had once been a Hollywood publicist. But after marrying Jeremy, she'd created and put all her energy into a non-profit called All Smiles, which raised money for the children's surgeries and coordinated all of their pre- and post-op care.

They'd been married for seven years. Neither had an arrest record. There was no known history of marital discord, nor of drug or alcohol abuse. On paper at least, they were the perfect couple. Keri was immediately suspicious.

After several wrong turns, she finally pulled up to the house at the end of Tower Road at 1:41, eleven minutes late.

To call it a house was an understatement. It was more of a compound on a property that seemed to cover several acres. From her vantage point, she could see the entire city of Los Angeles splayed out below her.

Keri took a moment to do something rare for her—put on extra makeup. Removing the sling had helped her appearance, but the yellowish bruise near her eye was still noticeable. So she dabbed it with some concealer until it was almost invisible.

Satisfied, she pushed the buzzer next to the security gate. As she waited for a response, she noticed Detective Frank Brody's maroon and white Cadillac parked in the roundabout.

A female voice came over the gate intercom.

"Detective Locke?"

"Yes."

"I'm Lupe Veracruz, the Burlingames' housekeeper. Please enter and park next to your partner. I'll meet you and take you to him and Dr. Burlingame."

The gate opened and Keri eased in, parking next to Frank's immaculately maintained vehicle. The Caddy was his baby. He was proud of its outdated color scheme, its poor gas mileage, and its whale-like size. He called it a classic. To Keri, the car, like its owner, was a dinosaur.

As she opened her car door, a petite, pleasant-looking Hispanic woman in her late forties came out to meet her. Keri got out of the car quickly, not wanting to let the woman see her struggle to navigate around her injured right shoulder. From this point on, Keri considered herself on enemy territory and at a potential crime scene. She didn't want to betray any sense of weakness to Burlingame or anyone in his orbit.

"This way, Detective," Lupe said, getting straight to business as she turned on her heel and led Keri along a cobblestone path, surrounded by immaculately manicured flowers. Keri tried to keep up while stepping carefully. With the injuries to her eye, shoulder, and ribs, she still felt uncertain on uneven ground.

They passed a huge pool with two diving boards and a lap lane. Next to it was a large pit, with a massive pile of dirt beside it. A Bobcat excavator sat idle nearby. Lupe saw her curiosity.

"The Burlingames are having a hot tub put in. But the Moroccan tile they ordered is on hold so the whole project is delayed."

"I'm having the same problem," Keri said. Lupe didn't laugh.

After several minutes, they reached a side entrance to the main house, which led into a large, airy kitchen. Keri could hear male voices nearby. Lupe directed her around the corner to what looked to be the breakfast room. Detective Brody was standing, facing in her direction, speaking to a man with his back to her.

The man seemed to sense her arrival and turned around before Lupe had the chance to announce her. Keri, in full investigative mode, focused on his eyes as he took her in. They were brown and warm, with just a hint of redness around the rims. He either had bad allergies or he'd been crying recently. He forced an awkward smile to his face, seemingly trapped between the expected responsibility to be a good host and the anxiety of the situation.

He was a nice-looking man, not quite attractive but with an open, friendly face that gave him an eager, boyish quality. Despite his sport coat, Keri could tell he was in good shape. He wasn't overtly muscular but had the lean wiry frame of an endurance athlete, maybe a marathoner or a triathlete. He was of average height, maybe five foot ten, and about 170 pounds. His short-cropped brown hair had the first, tiniest hints of gray.

"Detective Locke, thank you for coming," he said, walking forward and extending his hand. "I've just been speaking to your colleague."

"Keri," Frank Brody said, nodding curtly. "We haven't gotten into any details yet. I wanted to wait until you arrived."

It was subtle dig about her lateness masked by what seemed like professional courtesy. Keri, pretending not to notice, kept her focus on the doctor.

"Nice to meet you, Dr. Burlingame. I'm sorry it's under such difficult circumstances. If you don't mind, why don't we get started right away? In a missing persons case, every minute is crucial."

Out of the corner of her eye, Keri saw Brody scowl, clearly annoyed that she had taken over. She didn't really give a shit.

"Of course," Burlingame said. "Where should we begin?"

"You gave us a rough outline of the timeline over the phone. But I'd like you to walk us through it in more detail if you could. Why don't you start with the last time you saw your wife?"

Okay, it was yesterday morning and we were in the bedroom—"

Keri jumped in.

"I'm sorry to interrupt, but can you take us there? I'd like to be in the room as you describe the events that occurred there."

"Yes, of course. Should Lupe come as well?"

"We'll speak to her separately," Keri said. Jeremy Burlingame nodded and led the way up the stairs to the bedroom. Keri continued to watch him closely. Her interruption a moment earlier was only in part for the reason she gave.

She also wanted to gauge how a well-regarded, powerful doctor reacted to being repeatedly ordered around by a female. At least so far, it didn't seem to faze him. He appeared willing to do or say whatever she asked of him if it would help.

As they walked she peppered him with additional questions.

"Under normal circumstances, where would your wife be right now?"

"Here in the house, I imagine, preparing for tonight's fundraiser."

"What fundraiser is that?" Keri asked, feigning ignorance.

"We have a foundation that funds reconstructive surgery, mostly for children with facial irregularities, but sometimes for adults recovering from burns or accidents. Kendra runs the foundation and holds two major galas a year. One was scheduled for tonight at the Peninsula Hotel."

"Is her car here at the house?" Brody asked as they started up a long flight of stairs.

"I honestly don't know. I can't believe it didn't occur to me to check. Let me ask Lupe."

He took out his cell phone and used what appeared to be a walkie-talkie function.

"Lupe, do you know if Kendra's car is in the garage?" The response was almost immediate.

"No, Dr. Burlingame. I checked when you called earlier. It's not there. Also, I noticed one of her small travel bags was missing from her closet when I was hanging some clothes."

Burlingame looked perplexed.

"That's odd," he said.

"What is?" Keri asked.

"I just don't see why she would have had reason to take a travel bag anywhere. She has a duffel that she uses when she goes to the gym and she uses a garment bag if she plans to change into a gown at a gala location. She only uses the travel bags as carry-ons when we're actually traveling."

After climbing the flight of stairs and going down a long hallway, they reached the master bedroom. Brody, winded from the long trip, put his hands on his hips, stuck his chest out, and breathed in heavily.

18

Keri took the room in. It was enormous, bigger than her entire houseboat all by itself. The four-poster king bed was made. A willowy, sheer canopy surrounded it, making it look like a square cloud. The large balcony, with its door wide open, faced west, offering a view of the Pacific Ocean.

A massive flat-screen TV, easily seventy-five inches, hung on one wall. The other walls were tastefully decorated with paintings and photos of the happy couple. Keri walked over to look at one.

They seemed to be on vacation, somewhere warm with an ocean in the background. Jeremy wore an untucked, wrinkle-free button-down pink shirt with fitted plaid shorts. He had on sunglasses and his smile was slightly goofy and forced, that of a man uncomfortable having his picture taken.

Kendra Burlingame wore a turquoise sundress with stacked, block-heeled cage sandals that looped around her ankles. Her tanned skin popped against the dress. Her black hair was tied in a loose ponytail and her sunglasses rested on her head. She wore a broad smile, as if she'd just been laughing and had only barely managed to contain it. She was as tall as her husband, with long legs and aquamarine eyes that matched the water behind her. She was leaning into him and his arm was casually wrapped around her trim waist. She was stunningly beautiful.

"So the last time you saw your wife was when?" she asked. Her back was to Burlingame but she could see his reflection in the glass frame.

"In here," he said, his worried face hiding nothing from what she could tell. "It was yesterday morning. I had to leave early to go to San Diego to supervise a complicated procedure. She was still in bed when I kissed her goodbye. It was probably around six forty-five."

"Was she awake when you left?" Brody asked.

"Yes. She had the TV on. She was watching the local news to see what the weather would be like for tonight's gala."

"And that's the last time you saw her, yesterday morning?" Keri asked again.

"Yes, Detective," he said, sounding slightly annoyed for the first time. "I've answered that question several times now. May I ask you a question?"

"Of course."

"I know we have to go through everything methodically here. But in the meantime, can you please have your people check the GPS in Kendra's phone and car? Maybe that will help locate her."

19

Keri had been waiting for him to ask this question. Of course, Hillman had ordered the techs back at the station to begin that process the moment they got the case. But she'd been holding that detail back for this very moment. She wanted to gauge his response to her answer.

"It's a good idea, Dr. Burlingame," she said, "which is why we've already done it."

"And what did you find?" Burlingame asked hopefully.

"Nothing."

"Nothing? How could there be nothing?"

"It would appear that in both the phone and the car, the GPS has been turned off."

Keri, on full alert, watched closely for Burlingame's reaction.

He stared at her, stunned.

"Turned off? How is that possible?"

"It's only possible if it was done intentionally, by someone who didn't want either the phone or the car to be found."

"Does that mean it was a kidnapper who didn't want her found?"

"That's possible," Brody answered. "Or it could be that *she* didn't want to be found."

Burlingame's expression went from stunned to disbelieving.

"Are you suggesting that my wife left on her own and tried to hide where she was going?"

"It wouldn't be the first time," Brody said.

"No. That doesn't make any sense. Kendra isn't the kind of person to do that. Besides, she had no reason to. Our marriage is good. We love each other. She loves her work for the foundation. She loves those kids. She wouldn't just up and abandon all of that. I would know if there was something wrong. I would know."

To Keri's ear, he sounded almost pleading, like a man trying to convince himself. He looked utterly lost.

"Are you sure about that, Doctor?" she asked him. "Sometimes we keep secrets, even from the ones we love. Is there someone else she might have confided in, other than you?"

Burlingame seemed not to hear her. He sat down on the end of the bed, shaking his head slowly, as if that might somehow drive the doubt from his mind.

"Dr. Burlingame?" Keri asked again softly.

"Um, yeah," he said, rousing himself. "Her best friend is Becky Sampson. They've known each other since college. They went to a high school reunion together a couple of weeks ago and Kendra seemed a little rattled after she came back but wouldn't say why.

She lives off Robertson. Maybe Kendra mentioned something to her."

"All right, we'll get in touch with her," Keri assured him. "In the meantime, we're going to have a crime scene unit come in and do a thorough rundown of your house. We'll follow up on the last known location of your wife's car and phone before the GPS was disabled. Are you hearing me, Dr. Burlingame?"

The man appeared to have gone into a numbed stupor, staring straight ahead. At the sound of his name, he blinked and seemed to return to the moment.

"Yes, crime scene unit, GPS check. I understand."

"We'll also need to verify everything about your whereabouts yesterday, including your time in San Diego," Keri said. "We'll need to contact everyone you dealt with down there."

"We just have to do our due diligence," Brody added, in a clunky attempt to be diplomatic.

"I understand. I'm sure the husband is usually the main suspect when a woman disappears. It makes sense. I'll make a list of everyone I interacted with and give you their numbers. Do you need that now?"

"The sooner the better," Keri said. "I don't mean to be harsh but you're right, Doctor—the husband is typically a prime suspect. And the sooner we can eliminate you as one, the quicker we can move on to other theories. We're going to have some officers come out and secure the entire area. In the interim, I'd appreciate it if you and Lupe could join us in the courtyard where Detective Brody and I parked. We'll wait there until backup can arrive and CSU can begin processing the scene."

Burlingame nodded and shuffled out of the room. Then, suddenly, his head popped up and he asked a question.

"How long does she have, Detective Locke, assuming she was taken? I know there's a ticking clock on these things. How much time do you realistically think she has?"

Keri looked at him hard. There was no guile in his expression. He seemed to genuinely be clinging to something rational and factual to hold on to. It was a good question and one she needed to answer for herself.

She did some quick mental math. The numbers she came up with weren't good. But she couldn't be that blunt with a potential victim's husband. So she softened it a bit without lying.

"Look, Doctor. I'm not going to lie to you. Every second counts. But we still have a couple of days before the evidence trail starts to grow cold. And we're going to pour major resources into finding your wife. There's still hope."

But internally, the calculation was much less encouraging. Usually, seventy-two hours was the outer limit. So assuming she was taken sometime yesterday morning, they had a little less than forty-eight hours to find her. And that was being optimistic.

CHAPTER FIVE

Keri walked down the Cedars-Sinai Medical Center hallway as quickly as her aching body would allow. Becky Sampson's house was only blocks away from the hospital so Keri didn't feel too guilty about making a quick pit stop to check on Ray.

But as she approached his room, she could feel the recent, familiar nervousness start to churn in her gut. How were they going to make things normal between them again, when there was this silent secret they shared but couldn't acknowledge? As she reached his room, Keri resolved on what she hoped would be a temporary solution. She'd fake it.

The door was open and she could see that Ray was asleep. There was no one else in the room. The latest labor contract with the city stipulated that hospitalized officers got private rooms whenever available, so he had it pretty sweet. The room had a view of the Hollywood Hills and a big-screen TV, which was on but muted. Some old movie with Sylvester Stallone competing in an arm-wrestling competition filled the screen.

No wonder he fell asleep.

Keri walked over and studied her sleeping partner. Lying in bed, with a floral hospital gown loose about his body, Ray Sands looked much more frail than usual. Normally his six-foot-four, 230-pound African-American frame was intimidating, as was his completely bald head. He'd more than earned his sometime nickname of "Big."

With his eyes closed, his right glass eye, the one he'd lost in a boxing match years ago, wasn't noticeable. No one would guess that the forty-year-old man now lying in a hospital bed with an untouched bowl of red Jell-O next to him had once been Ray "The Sandman" Sands, an Olympic bronze medalist and professional heavyweight contender once considered a frontrunner to win the title. Of course, that was before an underrated southpaw with a brutal left hook had destroyed his eye and ended his career at age twenty-eight with one punch.

After flailing about for a while, Ray found policing and worked his way up to become one of the most highly regarded Missing Persons investigators in the department. And with Brody's imminent retirement, he was in line to take over his position in Robbery-Homicide.

Keri glanced out at the distant hills, wondering what their status would be in six months, when they were no longer partners or even in the same unit. She pushed the thought away, unwilling to imagine life without the one steadying influence in her life since Evie was taken.

Suddenly she sensed she was being watched. She glanced down and saw that Ray was awake, quietly staring at her.

"How's it going, Smurfette?" he asked playfully. They loved teasing each other about their dramatic size difference.

"Okay, how are you feeling today, Shrek?"

"A little tired, to be honest. I had a big workout a while ago. I walked all the way down the hallway and back. Look out, LeBron James, I'm on your heels."

"Did they give you a timetable for when they're letting you out?" she asked.

"They said maybe end of the week, if things keep progressing. Then it will be two weeks of bed rest at home. If that goes well, I'll be allowed to assume desk duty on a limited basis. Assuming I haven't shot *myself* from boredom before then."

Keri sat quietly for a moment, mulling over how to continue. Part of her wanted to tell Ray to take it slow, not to push too hard to get back to work. Of course, saying that would be hypocritical, as that was exactly what she'd done. And she knew he'd call her on it.

But he had been shot while helping save her life. She felt responsible. She felt protective of him. And she felt other things she wasn't quite prepared to think about at the moment.

Ultimately, she decided that giving him a distraction to focus on might be a better way to go than lecturing him.

"Along those lines, I could use your help with a case I just landed. You willing to mix in a little analysis with your Jell-O?" she asked.

"First of all, congrats on getting back on field duty. Second, how about we skip the Jell-O and go straight to the case?"

"Okay. Here are the basics. Kendra Burlingame, Beverly Hills socialite wife of a successful plastic surgeon, hasn't been heard from since yesterday morning—"

"What was yesterday again?" Ray interrupted. "The pain meds have me a little loopy when it comes to, you know, days of the week."

"Yesterday was Monday, Sherlock," Keri said snarkily. "Her husband says he last saw her at six forty-five a.m. before he went to San Diego to supervise a surgery. It's currently two forty on Tuesday afternoon, so that's about thirty-two hours missing."

"Assuming the husband's telling the truth. You know the first rule when it comes to missing wives—the husband did it."

24

Keri was annoyed that everyone, including her seemingly enlightened partner, seemed to constantly remind her of that. When she responded, she couldn't keep the sarcasm out of her voice.

"Really, Ray, is that the first rule? Let me write that one down because this is the first time I've heard it. Any other pearls of wisdom you care to offer, oh wise one? Maybe that the sun is hot? Or that kale tastes like aluminum foil?"

"I'm just saying—"

"Believe me, Ray, I know. And the guy is currently suspect number one. But she could have just run off too. I think that as a law enforcement professional, it might be worthwhile pursuing other leads, don't you?"

"I do. That way, you have a leg to stand on when you arrest him."

"Nice to see you using your keen investigative skills rather than just jumping to unfounded conclusions," Keri said mockingly, trying not to smile.

"That's how I roll. So what's next on the agenda?"

"I'm going to see Kendra's best friend when I leave here. Her place is just around the corner. The husband said Kendra was acting funny after the two of them returned from a high school reunion."

"Is anyone checking on the doctor's trip to San Diego?"

"Brody's headed down there now."

"You got partnered with Frank Brody on this?" Ray said, trying not to laugh. "No wonder you'd rather spend time with an invalid. How's that going?"

"Why do you think I didn't object when he offered to go to San Diego? The local guys down there could have just as easily followed up but he insisted and I figured it would keep him and his maroon atrocity of a car out of my way for a while. Besides, I'd rather spend time in the company of a worn-out, weak-muscled, bed-ridden sad sack like yourself than Brody any day."

All the banter had lulled Keri into a sense of comfort and she realized, too late, that her last comment had sent them right back to the awkward place. Ray was silent for a moment, then opened his mouth to speak but Keri got there first.

"Anyway, I should be heading out. I was supposed to be meeting Kendra's friend right about now. I'll check in with you later. Take it slow, okay?"

She left without waiting for a response. As she rushed down the hall to catch the elevator, she kept repeating one word over and over again.

Idiot. Idiot. Idiot.

25

CHAPTER SIX

Still feeling flushed with embarrassment, Keri drove the short distance to Becky Sampson's house. She caught sight of her blushing face in the rearview mirror and looked away quickly, trying to think of anything other than how she'd left things with Ray. It occurred to her that she'd rushed out so quickly, she forgot to tell him about the anonymous call regarding Evie and her trip to the abandoned warehouse.

This case, Keri. Keep your mind on this case.

She considered calling Detective Kevin Edgerton, the tech expert who was tracing Kendra's last known GPS location, to see if he'd had any luck.

Part of her was annoyed that having Edgerton work on this was taking him away from trying to break the code on Alan Pachanga's laptop. Again, frustration coursed through her as she remembered how they had initially thought they'd accessed an entire network of abductors, only to hit wall after wall.

Keri was certain that the cipher she needed was somewhere in the files of Pachanga's lawyer, Jackson Cave. She resolved that she was going to pay Cave a visit today, case or not.

As she made that pledge, she pulled up to Becky Sampson's place.

Time to set Cave aside for now. Kendra Burlingame needs my help. Stay focused.

She got out of her car and took in the neighborhood as she walked up to the main door of the apartment complex. Becky Sampson lived in a three-story Tudor-style building. The entire street, North Stanley Drive, was lined with similarly faux-ornate complexes.

This part of Beverly Hills, just south of Cedars-Sinai and Burton Way and west of Robertson Boulevard, was technically within the city limits. But as it was surrounded by commercial districts and abutting the city of Los Angeles, rent was significantly lower than in other sections of town. Still, the mailing address said Beverly Hills and that had its perks.

Keri buzzed Becky's unit and was let in right away. Once she was inside, it became apparent that the zip code was the major selling point of the place. It certainly wasn't the actual building. As she walked down the hall to the elevator, Keri took in the peeling light pink paint on the walls and the thick, mottled carpeting. Everything smelled moldy.

The elevator smelled even worse, like it had suffered through multiple vomit-related incidents over the years and could no longer hide the scent. It jerked unsteadily up until it reached the third floor and the doors rattled open. Keri stepped out, deciding to take the stairs on the way down, even if her ribs and shoulder would hate her for it.

She knocked on the door to unit 323, undid the clasp on her weapon, rested her hand over it unobtrusively, and waited. The sound of dishes being dumped unceremoniously in a sink was easy to identify, as was the thud as whatever had been lying on the floor was tossed in a closet.

Now she's checking herself in a mirror near the front door. There's the shadow across the peephole as she checks me out and the door should open in three, two...

Keri heard a lock turn and the door opened to reveal a thin, harried-looking woman. She must have been about the same age as Kendra if they'd gone to a reunion together but she looked much older, closer to fifty than forty. Her hair was a mousy brown, clearly dyed, and her brown eyes were as bloodshot as Keri's usually were. The word that immediately came to mind to describe her was jumpy.

"Becky Sampson?" she asked by way of protocol, although the driver's license photo she'd been sent en route clearly matched. Her right hand continued to rest on the butt of her gun.

"Yes. Detective Locke? Come on in."

Keri stepped inside, keeping some distance between her and Becky. Even rail-thin Beverly Hills wannabes could do damage if you let your guard down. She tried not to scrunch her nose up at the musty scent that dominated the place.

"Can I offer you anything?" Becky asked.

"I'd love a glass of water," Keri answered, less because she wanted one than because it allowed her to more fully take in the apartment while her hostess was in the kitchen.

With windows closed and the blinds drawn, the unit felt suffocating. Everything seemed to have a layer of dust on it, from the end tables to the bookshelves to the couch. Keri stepped into the living room and noticed that she was mistaken.

One part of the coffee table was shiny, as if it was in constant use. On the floor in front of that spot, Keri noticed several specks of what looked like white powder. She knelt down, ignoring the screaming pain in her ribs, and glanced under the table. She could see a partially rolled up one-dollar bill, covered in whitish residue.

27

She heard the water faucet turn off and stood up before Becky reentered the room with two glasses of water.

Clearly surprised to see her guest so far away from the front door, Becky gave her a suspicious look before involuntarily glancing down at the clear spot on the table.

"You mind if I sit down?" Keri asked casually. "I've got a broken rib and it hurts to stand for too long."

"Sure," Becky said, seemingly placated. "How did that happen?"

"A child kidnapper beat me up."

Becky's eyes widened in shock.

"Oh, don't worry," Keri reassured her. "I shot him to death after that."

Sufficiently confident that she had Becky off guard, she dove in.

"So I told you over the phone that I needed to talk to you about Kendra Burlingame. She's gone missing. Any idea where she might be?"

If possible, Becky's eyes widened even more than before.

"What?"

"She hasn't been heard from since yesterday morning. When is the last time you spoke to her?"

Becky tried to answer but suddenly began coughing and wheezing. After a few moments, she recovered enough to speak.

"We went shopping on Saturday afternoon. She was looking for a new dress for the fundraising gala tonight. Are you really sure she's missing?"

"We're sure. What was her demeanor like on Saturday? Did she seem anxious about anything?"

"Not really," Becky answered as she sniffed and reached for a tissue. "I mean, there were some minor hiccups with the fundraiser that she was dealing with, calls with caterers and so on. But it wasn't anything she hadn't dealt with a million times. She didn't seem that bothered."

"How was it for you, Becky, listening to her make those calls about a fancy gala while she bought an expensive dress?"

"What do you mean?"

"I mean, you're her best friend, right?"

Becky nodded. "For almost twenty-five years," she said.

"And she lives in a mansion up in the hills and you're in this one-bedroom apartment. You don't ever get jealous?"

She watched Becky closely as she answered. The other woman took a sip of her water, but coughed as if some of it had gone down the wrong pipe. After a few seconds, she answered.

"I do get jealous sometimes. I'll admit that. But it's not Kendra's fault that things haven't gone as well for me. Truthfully, it's hard to ever get upset with her. She's the nicest person I know. I've dealt with some…issues and she's always been there for me when things got rough."

Keri suspected what those "issues" might be but said nothing. Becky continued.

"Besides, she's very generous without lording it over me. That's a tough line to walk. She actually bought me the dress I'm wearing for the gala tonight, assuming it's even still happening. Do you know if it is?"

"I don't," Keri replied brusquely. "Tell me about her relationship with Jeremy. What was their marriage like?"

"It was good. They're great partners, a really effective team."

"That doesn't sound very romantic. Is it a marriage or a corporation?"

"I don't think they were ever a super-passionate couple. Jeremy's a very buttoned-down, matter-of-fact kind of guy. And Kendra went through her sexy, wild-guy phase in her twenties. I think she was happy to have a stable, sweet guy she could count on. I know she loves him. But it's not Romeo and Juliet or anything, if that's what you mean."

"Okay, so did she ever long for that passion? Could she have maybe gone looking for it, say on a high school reunion trip?" Keri asked.

"Why do you ask that?"

"Jeremy said that she seemed a little rattled after she returned from yours."

"Oh, that," Becky said, sniffing again before breaking out in another brief coughing fit.

As she tried to regain control, Keri noticed a cockroach scurry across the floor and tried to ignore it. When Becky recovered, she continued.

"Trust me, she wasn't messing around on the trip. In fact, it was the opposite. An ex-boyfriend of hers, a guy named Coy Brenner, kept coming on to her. She was polite but he was pretty relentless."

"How relentless?"

"Like, to the point of being uncomfortable. He was one of those wild guys I told you about. Anyway, he just wouldn't take no for an answer. At the end of the reunion, he said something about looking her up in town. I think it really got to her."

"Does he live here?"

"He lived in Phoenix for a long time. That's where the reunion was. We all grew up there. But he mentioned something about moving to San Pedro recently—said he was working down at the port."

"How long ago was this reunion?"

"Two weeks," Becky said. "Do you really think he had something to do with this?"

"I don't know. But we'll run it down. Where can I find you if I need to get in touch again?"

"I work at a casting agency over on Robertson, across from The Ivy. It's about a ten-minute walk from here. But I always have my cell. Please don't hesitate to call. Anything I can do to help, just ask. She's like a sister to me."

Keri looked hard at Becky Sampson, trying to decide whether to call her on the elephant in the room. The constant sniffing and coughing, the total disregard for maintaining a livable home, the white residue and rolled up bill on the floor all suggested that the woman was deep into cocaine addiction.

"Thanks for your time," she finally said, deciding to hold off for now.

Becky's situation might prove useful later. But there was no need to use it yet, when it served no tactical advantage. Keri left the apartment and took the stairs down, despite the jarring twinges in her shoulder and ribs.

She felt slightly guilty for keeping Becky's coke problem as a potential card to play down the road. But the guilt faded quickly as she left the building and breathed in the fresh air. She was a police detective, not a drug counselor. Anything that could help her solve the case was fair game.

As she pulled out into traffic and headed for the freeway, she called into the office. She needed everything they had on Kendra's aggressively interested ex-boyfriend, Coy Brenner. She was about to pay him an unannounced visit.

CHAPTER SEVEN

Keri tried to keep her cool even as she felt her blood pressure rising. Rush hour traffic was starting to back up as she made her way south on the 110 to the Port of Los Angeles in San Pedro. It was after four in the afternoon and even using the carpool lane and her siren, progress was slow.

She finally got off the freeway and wended her way through the complicated basin roads to the administration building on Palos Verdes Street. There she was supposed to meet her port police liaison, who would assign her two officers as backup when she interviewed Brenner. Port police participation was required since she was in their jurisdiction.

Normally Keri chafed at that kind of bureaucratic requirement but for once she didn't mind having backup. She usually felt pretty confident going up against any possible suspect, as she was trained in Krav Maga and had even taken some boxing lessons from Ray. But with her gimpy shoulder and battered ribs, she wasn't as sure of herself as usual. And Brenner didn't sound like a pushover.

According to Detective Manny Suarez back at the precinct, who ran a background check for Keri while she was on the road, Coy Brenner was a piece of work. He'd been arrested a half dozen times over the years, twice for drunk driving, once for theft, twice for assault, and most impressively for fraud, which had earned him his longest stint behind bars, six months. That was four years ago and since he wasn't allowed to leave the state for five, he was technically in violation of his parole.

Now he was a dockworker at pier 400. Even though he'd hinted to Becky and Kendra that he'd just moved to San Pedro in the last few weeks, records showed that he'd been living in a Long Beach apartment for over three months.

The port police liaison, Sergeant Mike Covey, and his two officers were waiting for her when she arrived. Covey was a tall, thin balding man in his late forties with a no-guff demeanor to him. She'd briefed him over the phone and he'd obviously done the same with his men.

"Brenner's shift ends at four thirty," Covey told her after they'd exchanged introductions. "Since it's already four fifteen, I called the pier manager and told him not to let the crew out early. He's been known to do that."

"I appreciate it. I guess we should head right over. I want to get a look at the guy before I interview him."

"Understood. If you want, we can take your car over first to arouse less suspicion. Officers Kuntsler and Rodriguez can follow separately in the squad car. We patrol the piers constantly so having them in the area won't seem odd to your suspect. But if he sees an unfamiliar face get out of one of our vehicles, it might raise eyebrows."

"That sounds good," Keri agreed, appreciative that she wasn't facing a turf war. She knew it was likely because the port police hated bad publicity. They would happily dispose of this thing quietly, even if meant ceding authority to another agency.

Keri followed Sergeant Covey's directions across the Vincent Thomas Bridge and to the visitor parking area for pier 400. It took longer than Keri expected and they arrived at 4:28. Covey spoke into the radio, telling the pier manager he could release the crew.

"Brenner should walk right across our line of sight to the employee parking area any minute," he said. As he spoke, the squad car passed by them and started a long, slow casual loop along the road circling the pier. It seemed completely unremarkable.

Keri watched the dockworkers file out of the pier warehouse. One guy realized he'd left his hardhat on and jogged back to return it. Two others ran across the broad expanse, clearly racing each other to their cars. The rest walked in a large group, apparently in no hurry.

"There's your guy," Covey said, nodding in the direction of the one guy walking alone. Coy Brenner bore only a passing resemblance to the man in the mug shot from his arrest in Arizona four years earlier. That man had a lean and hungry look, with longish, shaggy brown hair and a hint of stubble.

The guy lumbering across the parking lot now had put on about twenty pounds in the intervening years. His hair was cropped short and his stubble was now a full-on beard. He wore blue jeans and a lumberjack-style shirt and walked with his head down and a grimace on his face. Coy Brenner didn't strike her as a man happy with his lot in life.

"Can you hang back, Sergeant Covey? I want to see how he reacts when confronted solo by a female cop."

"Sure. I'll head over to the warehouse for now. I'll tell the boys to stay back as well. Give a wave when you want us to join you."

"Will do."

Keri got out of her car, threw on a blazer to hide her gun, and followed Brenner from a distance, not wanting to make her presence known just yet. He seemed oblivious to her, lost in his own thoughts. By the time he reached his old pickup truck, she was almost on him. She felt her phone buzz with a text and tensed up. But he obviously didn't hear it.

"How ya doin', Coy?" she asked coquettishly.

He spun around, clearly taken by surprise. Keri removed her sunglasses, gave him a broad smile, and placed her hand on her hip playfully.

"Hi?" he asked more than said.

"Don't tell me you don't remember me? It's only been about fifteen years. You are Coy Brenner from Phoenix, right?"

"Yeah. Did we go to school together or something?"

"No. Our time together was educational, but not in a school kind of way, if you know what I mean. I'm starting to get offended a little bit here."

I'm really laying it on thick here. Maybe I've lost my touch.

But Coy's face softened and Keri could tell she'd hit pay dirt.

"Sorry—long day and lots of years," he said. "I'd be happy to get reacquainted. What was your name again?" He seemed genuinely perplexed.

"Keri. Keri Locke."

"I'm really surprised that I can't place you, Keri. You seem like the kind of girl I'd remember. What are you doing all the way out here?"

"I can't stand the heat back in Arizona. I work for the city now. Case work—kind of boring. What about you?"

"You're looking at what I do."

"A boy from the desert ends up working by the water. What made that happen? Looking to break into the movies? Wanted to learn to surf? Following a girl?"

She kept the tone light but watched closely for his reaction to that last question. His bemused but intrigued expression immediately disappeared, replaced by one of wariness.

"I'm really having trouble placing you, Keri. Remind me again when we hung out?" There was a sharpness to his tone that hadn't been there a moment before.

Keri could sense her ruse was wearing thin and decided to poke a little more aggressively.

"Maybe you don't remember me because I don't look like Kendra. Is that it, Coy? You only have eyes for her?"

Those eyes turned quickly from wary to angry and he took a step forward. Keri watched his fists clench involuntarily. She didn't flinch.

"Who the hell are you?" he demanded. "What is this?"

33

"I'm just making conversation, Coy. Why so rude all of a sudden?"

"I don't know you," he said, now outright hostile. "Who sent you, her husband? Are you some kind private investigator?"

"What if I was? Would I have something to investigate? Is there something you want to get off your chest, Coy?"

He took another step toward her. Their faces were less than a foot apart now. Rather than shrink, Keri squared her shoulders and lifted her chin defiantly.

"I think you've made a terrible mistake coming here, lady," Coy growled. His back was to the squad car, which had slowly rolled up behind him and was now idling twenty feet away.

Out of the corner of her eye, Keri could see Sergeant Covey cautiously making his way over from the warehouse, careful to stay behind Coy as well. She felt a sudden urge to wave in their direction but forced the feeling down.

It's now or never.

"What did you do to Kendra, Coy?" she demanded, any trace of playfulness gone from her voice. She stared hard at him, hand once again brushing the butt of her gun, ready for anything.

At her question, his eyes went from angry to surprised and she could tell he had no idea what she was talking about. He took a step back.

"What?"

She immediately sensed that he wasn't the guy, but pressed on just in case.

"Kendra Burlingame has gone missing and I hear you're her personal stalker. So if you've done something to her, now would be the time to come clean. If you cooperate, I can help you. If you don't, it could get very bad for you."

Coy was staring at her but he didn't seem to be fully processing what she said. He was oblivious to Sergeant Covey moving to within a few steps behind him. The veteran officer's hand rested on his gun hip. He didn't look trigger-happy, just prepared.

"Kendra's missing?" Coy asked, sounding like a kid who'd just learned his dog had been put down.

"When's the last time you saw her, Coy?"

"The reunion—I told her I would look her up here in LA. But I could tell she didn't want any part of me. She looked embarrassed for me. I didn't want to see that look on her face again so I just dropped it."

"You didn't want to punish the woman who made you feel that way?"

"She didn't make me feel that way. I'm ashamed of what I've become without any help from her. It was just seeing how far I'd fallen in her view—it was a real eye-opener, you know? I've been lying to myself about being this cool, tough guy for a long time. It took Kendra for me to see myself as the loser I really am."

He looked at her desperately, hoping to make some kind of connection. But Keri didn't feel like exploring this guy's inner demons. She had enough shame of her own that she didn't want to deal with someone else's.

"Can you account for your whereabouts yesterday, Coy?" she asked, changing the subject. Realizing he wasn't going to get any sympathy from her, he nodded.

"I was here all day. I'm sure my boss can verify it."

"We can check on that," Sergeant Covey said. Coy jumped slightly at the unexpected voice behind him. He turned around, surprised to see Covey within feet of him and the squad car with Kuntsler and Rodriguez not much farther away.

"So I guess you're a cop, then?" Coy said, looking downtrodden.

"I am—LAPD Missing Persons."

"I hope you find her. Kendra's a great gal. The world's a better place because of her and she deserves to be happy. I always held a torch for her. But I knew she was out of my league so I never got my hopes up. If there's anything else I can do to help, let me know."

"Detective Locke," Sergeant Covey interjected, "unless you have additional questions, I'm happy to follow up on his alibi. I know you have other avenues of investigation you want to explore. Besides, we need to do some paperwork to process Mr. Brenner for separation. He lied on his application about his parole status and that's cause for termination."

Keri saw Brenner's face sag even more. He was truly pathetic. And now he was unemployed on top of it. She tried to shake away the feeling that she was partly responsible for that.

"I'd appreciate that, Sergeant. I do need to get back and this looks like a dead end. Thanks for all your help."

As Covey and the officers led Coy Brenner back to the warehouse for interrogation, Keri got in her car and checked the text she received earlier.

It was from Brody. It read:

GALA STILL ON. GREAT CHANCE FOR INTERVIEWS. MEET YOU THERE. DRESS SEXY.

Brody continued to amaze her with his lack of insight and professionalism. In addition to being an unrepentant sexist, he didn't seem to get that a fundraiser whose hostess was missing wasn't the ideal venue to get her friends and colleagues to bare their souls.

Besides that, I don't even have anything to wear.

Of course, that wasn't the only reason. If she was being honest with herself, Keri had to admit that part of her dread was because this was exactly the sort of event she went to all the time back when she was a respected professor, the wife of a successful talent agent, and the mother of an adorable little girl. Going to this thing would be a bright, shiny, painful reminder of her life before she lost Evie.

Sometimes she hated this job.

CHAPTER EIGHT

Keri's stomach was a churning pit of anxiety as she sat in the waiting room of Jackson Cave's law firm. He'd made her wait twenty minutes already, long enough for her to repeatedly rethink whether this was a good decision.

She'd been on the way back from San Pedro, calculating how long it would take her to get to the houseboat to change into an evening gown and then to Beverly Hills for the All Smiles fundraiser. But as she headed north, she saw the skyscrapers of downtown Los Angeles in the distance and a powerful urge took over. She found herself driving to Cave's office, without any kind of plan to fall back on.

On the way there, she'd called Brody so they could debrief each other. After she filled him in on the Coy Brenner dead end, he told her about San Diego.

"Jeremy Burlingame's alibi checks out. He was in surgery all day yesterday. Apparently he was supervising some doctors down there, teaching them a new facial reconstruction procedure."

"All right, listen, traffic's a real bitch here," Keri said. It was partly true but also an excuse for her to stop at Cave's. "So if you get to the gala before me, please just scope the place out. Don't start interrogating people."

"Are you telling me how to do my job, Locke?"

"No, Brody. But I am suggesting that going into this place like a bull in a china shop might be counterproductive. Some of these socialite women would probably open up more to another chick in a dress than to a guy whose longest relationship has been with his car."

"Screw you, Locke. I'll talk to whoever I want," Brody said indignantly. But she could hear in his voice that he had doubts about how good an idea that was.

"Suit yourself," Keri replied. "See you there."

Now, a full half hour later, she still hadn't gotten in to see Cave. It was almost 5:30. She decided to take advantage of the lull to look around. She walked up to the reception desk.

"Do you know how much longer Mr. Cave is going to be?" she asked the secretary, who shook her head apologetically. "Then can you tell me where the restroom is, please?"

"Down the hall to the left."

Keri headed that way, her eyes alert for any detail that could work to her advantage. Directly across from the women's restroom was a door marked Exit. She opened it and saw that it opened into the same hallway she'd come down to get to the main entrance of the firm.

Glancing around and seeing no one in the hall, she pulled a tissue out of her purse and shoved it into the tube latch hole so that it couldn't lock automatically. Then she stepped into the restroom briefly for the sake of appearance.

When she returned to the lobby, an attractive woman in a crisp business suit was waiting to lead her to Jackson Cave's office. As she followed the woman, she tried to keep her heart from beating out of her chest. She was about to meet with the man who might hold the key to getting crucial information about Evie's whereabouts and she had no game plan.

The only other time she'd met with Jackson Cave had been at a police station in a small mountain town. He'd come to try to bail out his client, Payton Penn, the brother of California Senator Stafford Penn. Ultimately, she discovered that Penn had hired Alan Pachanga to abduct his niece, Ashley. Things had gone her way back in that mountain town, but now she was in enemy territory and she could sense it.

Jackson Cave was known throughout most of the city for his reputation representing major corporate clients. But to law enforcement, his pro-bono work defending rapists, pedophiles, and child abductors was his claim to infamy.

Keri was immediately suspicious of a man like that. It was one thing to defend a murder suspect in a death row case or some desperate guy who robbed a bank to support his family. But to exclusively and enthusiastically represent the worst perpetrators of sexual violence that the city had to offer, free of charge, struck her as an odd choice.

Nonetheless, Keri hoped to put his work to her advantage. She knew that somewhere in Cave's possession must be a cipher that could crack the code to Alan Pachanga's computer. If she could find it, that could lead her to information on a whole network of abductors for hire. It might even include something about the man who'd taken Evie, a man she believed went by the name "The Collector."

Everything about the place was designed to intimidate. The firm itself consumed the entire seventieth floor of the seventy-three-story US Bank Tower. There were floor-to-ceiling windows everywhere, looking out on the vastness of Los Angeles. Expensive art covered the walls. All the furniture was leather and mahogany.

They finally reached an unmarked office at the end of the hall and the woman led her in. It was empty. Keri was directed to a plush chair across from Cave's desk, which was immaculate.

Left alone, she glanced around, trying to glean something about the man from his surroundings. There were no personal photos on his desk or credenza. On the wall were some photos of Cave with movers and shakers such as the mayor, several city councilmen, and a few celebrities. His college (USC) and law school (Harvard) diplomas were displayed as well. But nothing gave a sense of the man or his passions.

Before Keri could study the room further, Jackson Cave walked in. She stood up quickly. He was just as she remembered him from their last meeting. His coal black hair was slicked back like Gordon Gekko in *Wall Street*. His blindingly white teeth filled out a mouth twisted into a fake, plastic smile. His tan skin gleamed underneath his navy Michael Kors suit. And his penetrating blue eyes glinted with a fierceness that reminded her of an eagle hunting prey.

And then, in a flash, she knew her course of action. Jackson Cave, with his personal photos with power players and his immaculate grooming and attire, was a man who cared about how he was perceived. He made his living off winning people over— politicians, juries, the media. And Keri knew he wanted to win her over too. It was his nature.

I have to undermine that goal. I have to come at him hard and fast, upend his expectations, keep him off balance. The only way I'm going to poke through his armor and get him to slip up is if I jab him in enough places. Maybe then he'll say something inadvertently that could lead me to crack the cipher.

If she could get him upset, or even just annoyed, maybe he'd make a mistake and inadvertently reveal something important. Considering she already despised the man, it wasn't a big lift. She just had to amp it up and look for cracks in his perfect façade. She didn't know exactly what those cracks might be, but if she stayed alert, she was sure she'd find something.

"Detective Keri Locke," he said as he swept past her to his side of the desk, "what an unexpected surprise. It was only a few weeks ago that we chatting in the fresh mountain air. And now you've consented to visit me here in the concrete jungle. To what do I owe the honor?"

Before speaking, Keri took a step toward one of the photos of Cave with a local dignitary so that her back was to him. She did it partly to show that she was in charge of the meeting, partly to get under his skin by refusing to look at him directly, and partly

39

because her ribs were starting to ache again and she didn't want him to see her gritting her teeth in discomfort.

"Sorry to bother you, counselor. I know you must be busy, preparing to defend an accomplice to child abduction."

"Alleged, Detective. Alleged accomplice."

She ignored his comment and continued.

"I came down here to ask you a question. Why is it, with so many powerful corporate clients at your disposal, you insist on representing the dregs of society?"

She glanced casually over her shoulder as if she didn't have a care in the world but focused intently on Cave's eyes, looking for any sign of distress. He offered none. Clearly, he was used to these kinds of put-downs.

"Everybody deserves quality representation, Detective. It's in the constitution—sixth amendment. Look it up."

"I'm aware of that, Mr. Cave," she said, returning her attention to the wall of photos. "But you could represent any kind of defendant and yet you seem drawn to those who engage in violent behavior toward women and children. Why is that?"

"Something for me to work out with my therapist, I suppose." He sounded relaxed, completely unruffled.

This isn't working. He's too practiced at batting away attacks about his clients. I have to poke somewhere else.

"That's a cute quip, Mr. Cave. I'll bet it's one you use when defending your work to folks like him," she said, pointing at the city councilman in the photo she'd been looking at. She turned quickly to see his reaction and saw that he still seemed unfazed.

"Is this what you came here for, Detective—to try to guilt-trip me? How boring…and disappointing. I expected more of you."

"Sorry to disappoint. But I can't help wonder why these people aren't more reluctant to be seen with you. After all, isn't that the CEO of a major rape crisis center in that picture with you?" she asked, pointing to an older woman almost melting into Cave as he wrapped his arm around her.

"Lovely lady," he said, unperturbed. "Nice gams too."

"And this gentleman, the monsignor," Keri continued. "I'm wondering if he had to go to confession after meeting with you. Or at least take a Silkwood shower."

She was surprised that Cave didn't come back at her with another blasé reply. In fact, she noticed that he'd visibly tensed. The plastic smile still covered his face. But for the briefest of seconds she saw something in those blue eyes she couldn't quite identify.

He regrouped quickly, regaining his normal expression, and stepped around to her side of the desk.

"This has been wonderfully fun," he said, "but unfortunately, I still have a lot of work to do tonight. And unless you're here for some reason other than to attack my personal character, I'm going to have to end our little get-together."

He pushed a buzzer and the woman who had brought Keri in immediately appeared to take her away.

"This way please, ma'am," she said politely but firmly. "They can validate you at the front desk."

As she walked out the door, Cave called after her with an almost musical lilt in his voice.

"Don't be a stranger, Keri."

Oh, don't worry, you smug bastard, I won't. In fact, I plan to be back here again much sooner than you think.

Keri smiled to herself as she took the elevator downstairs. Even the prospect of driving across town to get a gown and then interrogate rich women looking down their noses at her didn't perturb her at that moment.

It didn't bother her because she had figured out what she had seen in Cave's eyes in that moment when she'd commented on the photo with the monsignor.

It was panic.

And it gave her the insight she needed.

Behind it, she knew, was the key to finding her daughter.

CHAPTER NINE

Keri stared at herself in the restroom mirror for what felt like the hundredth time. Her stomach was doing somersaults and her mouth was dry.

Outside the door, she could hear the fundraising gala attendees chatting away. But inside the family restroom near the Peninsula Hotel Verandah Ballroom, Keri Locke tried to convince herself that she could get away with wearing the form-fitting, one-shoulder black evening gown she had on. It was the one fancy dress she still had from her previous life.

She had taken off the rib-protecting wraps as there was no way she could fit into the dress with them on. Even if she could have, they would have made her look like the Stay Puft Marshmallow Man.

She had tied her hair back in a loose bun that looked dressier than her usual ponytail. She also wore a pair of short black heels, a concession to the event that would still allow her to move around without too much discomfort.

She stepped back for one last look.

Come on, Keri. You're here as a cop investigating a possible crime. You could show up at this thing in a camouflage pantsuit and these people would defer to you. You're doing this to blend in and keep people at ease. But you are in charge. Act like it.

With that in mind, she stepped out into the hall and made her way to the ballroom, armed with a list Becky Sampson had given her of Kendra's best friends among the socialite set. But before she could seek them out, she saw Brody across the room. Ignoring the string quartet in the middle of the room, she made her way past the staff serving small bites and champagne, and through the throng of tuxedos and cocktail dresses to meet him.

He was wearing the same rumpled, sauce-stained suit from this morning. Part of her admired that but another part thought it might be an impediment to getting these people's trust. She was pretty sure her instinct was right.

"I just got a call from that nerd Edgerton," he said without so much as a hello. "They traced the GPS on Kendra's car and phone to their last known location before they were both disabled—a bus station parking structure in Palm Springs. There was nothing incriminating in the car. Palm Springs PD is searching the area for any sign of her but hasn't found anything yet. They're checking video of the bus station and ticket sales to see if anything pops. But it's looking like Kendra Burlingame and her 'only for traveling' travel bag might have taken an actual trip, just one the doctor didn't know about."

Keri took in what Brody was saying as she looked around the elegant ballroom full of pretty people. It was hard to argue with his logic. But something about it didn't feel right.

Kendra Burlingame struck Keri as the kind of person who was fully committed to this organization. If she wanted to bail on her life, why not wait a day or two, until after she was sure the fundraiser had achieved its purpose? Why abandon her project before it was complete? It wasn't inconceivable but it didn't sit right.

"You may be right, Brody. But we're here, so we may as well play this out. Let's talk to folks to see why she might have wanted to cut and run or if they even think that's in her character."

Brody nodded his acquiescence.

"You want to take the chicks and I'll talk to the penguins?" he asked.

Keri nodded, not wanting to get into a dispute about gender stereotyping at the moment. Besides, everyone on Becky's list was a woman anyway.

She found the event manager, a mousy, frazzled woman wearing glasses that kept sliding down her nose, who matched names on paper to faces in the room for her. Then Keri began the hard work of interrogating a bunch of rich women about their missing friend while at that missing friend's charity event.

After about a half hour, it became clear that none of these women had any real insight into Kendra's personal life. All they could offer were pleasant platitudes and stock words of concern.

Right when she was about to give up, the event manager walked over and pointed out a woman in a tight, strapless red dress who had just walked in.

"That woman wasn't on your list but I know she and Mrs. Burlingame were close. In fact, she was here last week with her, helping coordinate details for the event."

"What's her name?"

"Margaret Merrywether—although she may tell you something different."

"What do you mean?"

"You'll find out. I'm sure she's a great friend, but to a girl like me, she's your basic nightmare."

"Thank you," Keri said and headed in Margaret's direction. As she approached her, she couldn't help but wonder why Becky had left her off the list. In fact, she realized that Becky wasn't even here yet. Maybe she was dealing with a cocaine-related delay.

The closer she got to Margaret Merrywether, the more she realized she was about to be dealing with a piece of work. The woman was tall, easily six feet, with porcelain white skin and flaming red hair that matched her dress.

Unlike the sophisticated but subdued evening gowns the other women wore, hers revealed her creamy white shoulders and a provocative, plunging neckline. Her black stiletto heels were easily six inches high. She looked like an elegant Amazon.

Keri looked up to discover that the woman's sharp green eyes were focused on her, a hint of a smile playing at her ruby red lips. She had caught Keri taking her in and they both knew it.

No point in playing coy at this point.

"Detective Keri Locke," she said, extending her hand. "I'm with LAPD's Missing Persons Unit."

"Well, it's about time," Margaret Merrywether said in a languid southern accent as she extended a long slender arm and shook Keri's hand delicately. "I've been expecting someone to reach out to me ever since I heard about Kenny. What took you so long?"

"We only just learned about your connection to Mrs. Burlingame, ma'am. Maybe you can fill me in a little more on your relationship to…Kenny, as you call her. Did she go by that nickname with everyone?"

"First of all, no, she did not. I'm the only one cheeky enough to get away with it. Second of all, Ms. Locke, please do not call me ma'am. Only my children do that and it's usually when they're in trouble. If you want to make me uncomfortable, you can call me Ms. Merrywether. If you want to make me sound like a cliché on a hot tin roof you can call me Maggie, like my ex-husband does. But if you want to call me what Kenny calls me, it's just Mags."

Keri, for the first time in a long time, wasn't sure how to react. She made it her business to predict human behavior for a living. She was a detective now and before that she'd been a professor of criminology. Rarely did someone truly surprise her. But this woman was like a twenty-first-century Scarlett O'Hara mixed with Jessica Rabbit. Keri decided to just keep it simple.

"Okay then. So how do you know Mrs. Burlingame, Ms. Merrywether?"

"Oh dear, so formal, so professional. I suppose I should be happy that the person looking into Kenny's disappearance is so unwavering. I'd imagine your cohort over there would be…less immune to my charms."

She nodded across the room to Brody, who was scarfing down stuffed mushrooms while leering unapologetically at two well-dressed women trying to pretend they didn't notice him.

"I wouldn't consider that a major achievement, Ms. Merrywether. Detective Brody could just as easily be charmed by a poster of Rosie the Riveter. I think he was a teenager around the time she was big."

"You are undermining my delicate sense of self-esteem, Detective Locke," Ms. Merrywether said, her voice full of faux offense.

"I find that very hard to believe. Now, as entertaining as you are, I really need some straight answers. If Kendr…er, Kenny, really is as close a friend as you say, then I'd expect you to be desperate to tell me everything you could."

"You're right, of course. I was just testing you a bit, Detective, to see if you were worthy of my time or if I should take what I know to someone in a position of greater authority."

"And did I pass your test?"

"You did indeed. Perhaps we can make our way somewhere a little more private where there are fewer prying eyes and eager ears."

"Lead the way," Keri said. As she followed Merrywether out of the ballroom, she saw Jeremy Burlingame entering from a different entrance. He looked to be headed toward the dais.

In his hands was a series of note cards, which he was fumbling with. Inevitably they spilled to the floor. He clumsily bent to pick them up, then awkwardly thanked the multiple people who rushed over to help him.

Margaret Merrywether was almost out of the room when Burlingame stepped up to the podium.

"Hold on a sec. I want to hear this," Keri said.

"So do I, actually," Ms. Merrywether agreed.

The music stopped and the room quieted as Burlingame cleared his throat loudly into the microphone.

"Um…sorry, er, give me a moment here," he said as he adjusted the height of the microphone stand, which had clearly been set up for Kendra. "I'm not great at this sort of thing. I know you're used to having my wife, Kendra, speak at these events. But as many of you have heard, she's missing."

There was an audible gasp in the room. Apparently at least some of the guests had been unaware. Burlingame continued.

"The police are searching diligently for her. And I'm very hopeful that she'll be found and returned safely to me. I would ask that if any of you know anything you think might be helpful, please inform the authorities immediately.

"As for me, I'm trying to keep from going stir crazy by staying busy. After I spoke to the detectives investigating Kendra's case, I returned to work and performed surgery this afternoon on an infant born with a facial abnormality.

"Part of me felt guilty—as if there was something else I could or should be doing to help with the search. But then I realized I was doing what Kendra would want. I'm not a detective. I'd probably just be in the way. And it wouldn't have helped that little boy for me to cancel his procedure. And then it hit me—I couldn't cancel this event either. It wouldn't help find Kendra any faster if I did. And kids like the one I helped today would have hundreds of thousands fewer dollars available to help defray the costs of these surgeries.

"Kendra and I—and let's be honest, it was mostly Kendra—created All Smiles to help disadvantaged children and others in need of reconstructive plastic surgery. And this event advances that goal. So I had to proceed, as awkward as it feels. Besides, when Kendra returns, she'd kill me if she learned I'd cancelled."

People in the ballroom laughed, then stopped suddenly, unsure if it was appropriate. Burlingame smiled weakly before continuing.

"So as much as I dislike public speaking and as uncomfortable as it is for me to be up here under these circumstances, I'm asking you to contribute generously tonight. It's what these children need. It's what Kendra would want. And when we find her—if she sees that you cheaped out—she's going to hunt you down. Thank you."

He stepped off the dais and was immediately surrounded by a swarm of well-wishers. The man looked completely overwhelmed. Keri had been hoping to talk to him again but that would have to wait.

She turned around to look for Margaret Merrywether, who had already left the ballroom and was walking down the hall in the direction of the hotel's Club Bar. She looked back over her shoulder and called out to Keri.

"Come on, Detective Locke," she purred. "Don't you want to know what's really going on?"

46

CHAPTER TEN

Keri's feet were killing her. Her ribs were screaming. And her shoulder throbbed dully. But she pretended all was well as the two women stood in the least crowded corner of the bar.

A waiter had offered them a tiny table but they declined, silently agreeing with a shared look that there was no way either of them could squeeze into such a tight space in their dresses.

Their drinks came quickly. Margaret ordered a scotch and soda. Keri, who thought that sounded desperately appealing, ordered a club soda and cranberry juice. She expected a look of disdain from the aristocrat next to her but none was forthcoming. Instead, she leaned over and whispered in Keri's ear.

"I have a secret to tell you, but I will only share it if you agree to call me Mags."

Keri was having trouble keeping up the professional façade in the midst of Merrywether's easy charm, the constant discomfort she was feeling, and the overpowering noise of the bar.

Life's too short to fight this battle.

"Okay, Mags, you win. What's your secret?"

"My feet are in agony and I'm taking off these heels, regardless of the consequences."

"I'll keep that secret if you'll keep mine."

"What's that, Detective?"

"Mine are off already. I dumped them the second you said 'feet.'"

"All right then," Mags said, as she bent down to pull hers off. "I'm actually surprised you kept yours on as long as you did. You don't strike me as the type to stand on ceremony."

"I'm not, Mags. And that's why I'm going to have to dispense with all the ladylike pleasantries and cut to the chase. What do you know? You didn't seem all that impressed with Jeremy Burlingame's speech up there."

"Oh, don't read too much into that, Detective. I'm not suspicious of Jeremy. I'm just bored with him. He may be a brilliant surgeon and a devoted husband, but I find him to be as interesting as human wallpaper."

"What kept Kendra so interested in him?"

"Who's to say she was?"

"What are you suggesting? That she—"

"Now don't get your undies in a bundle. I'm not casting aspersions. I just meant, well, why do you think she's thrown

47

herself so relentlessly into this foundation? Surely a large part of it is because she believes strongly in the cause. But remember, she also used to be a high-powered Hollywood publicist. Do you think that drive and passion just disappeared once she got married? I can assure you it did not."

"If she got bored enough, do you think she might have run off? Just left town without telling anyone?"

"Is that what you think happened? Is that what Jeremy thinks?" Mags asked. She sounded appalled by the idea.

"No. He's convinced she was abducted. And my inclination is to suspect that as well. But we've got conflicting evidence and a lot of it points to her just taking off."

"Look, Detective," Mags said, her voice as serious as Keri had heard it all night. "No one can be certain what's in another person's heart. We all keep a part of ourselves forever locked up to the world. But I've known Kendra Burlingame for over a decade, back when she was Kendra Ann Maroney, just off the turnip truck from Phoenix, Arizona. And nothing about the woman I know, about my dear friend, ever indicated that she was the type of person to just cut and run. It's not in her character. Kenny's a fighter, not a quitter. And I'm hoping that you'll fight for her too. I may put on a good show. But I'm very worried about her."

Keri took the comment in, surprised and heartened by Mags's ferocity. It gave her confidence that her own instincts weren't completely off the mark.

"Fair enough," she replied. "But you said earlier you could tell me what's really going on. So spill it, Mags. I know this must all seem very dramatic to you. But we're in a time crunch here. If Kenny really was taken as long ago as yesterday morning, we're at around the thirty-six-hour mark. Whoever did this had a big head start and the trail is getting colder every second. We need to follow up every possible lead as quickly as possible. So tell me what you've been holding back since we met."

Mags looked at her for a few seconds, clearly in the midst of some internal struggle. Keri could tell she'd made her decision when she took a big swig of her drink and swallowed hard.

"I'm telling you this in case it's important. But if you determine that it's not, I'd ask you to please keep it confidential. If it got out, it could do Kenny great harm. I only say it now because her safety is more important than her status. Do I have your word?"

"I promise that if what you tell me isn't relevant to the case, it won't go beyond me."

"That's good enough for me. When Kenny first moved to LA fifteen years ago, before she got into publicity, she wanted to be an actress. She took some head shots and the photographer offered her some extra money to take a few... more risqué photos. She was really struggling to make the rent so she did it."

Right at that moment, a guy wearing a gaudy silver suit sauntered up to them. He had *Miami Vice*–era stubble, a dyed-brown receding hairline he was trying to hide with a grisly comb-over, and the smell of a man who had recently bathed in cigarette smoke.

"Can I get either of you ladies a refill?" he asked forcefully. "Or maybe you'd like some fresh, organic liquid refreshment? I'm happy to provide some."

Keri stared at him, stunned that someone actually thought that line would work under any circumstances, much less in an environment like this. She started to speak but Mags raised her hand almost imperceptibly as if to say "I've got this," before turning to face the man directly.

"What's your name, you strapping sir?" she asked.

"Kyle."

"Kyle what?"

"Kyle Hinton."

"Kyle Hinton—it just rolls off the tongue, doesn't it, Keri?"

Keri nodded, curious to see where this was going next.

"Kyle," Mags continued, "if what you mean is that you would like to pay for another drink from the bar for one or both of us—why, that would be delicious. But if you're hinting that you'd like to present either of us with some 'liquid' of your own creation, I feel confident in declining on both our behalves. I can assure you that neither of us have any interest in engaging in sexual activity with you. Or in talking to you. Or even in being in your proximity any longer. Do you know what I mean, Kyle?"

"Fine, be that way," he said, realizing he was out of his depth. "Couldn't you just have said 'no thanks'?"

"I could have, Kyle. But how would that help the next lady to whom you offer fresh, organic liquid refreshment? Let this be a lesson to you, Kyle Hinton. There's no hiding for men like you anymore. Now be on your way."

Kyle stood there for a second, then, apparently done taking abuse for the night, turned and left without another word.

Keri watched him go, then looked back at Mags with awe.

"Can I take you along to some of my precinct meetings? I think you could really clean up the place."

"It would be my great honor."

The waiter came over to ask if they wanted another round, snapping Keri out of the moment and reminding her of her priorities.

"Not for me. But I would love a few Advil if you have some behind the bar."

"And I'll take a refill, darling," Mags told him. He nodded and walked off.

"So you were saying," Keri prompted.

Mags picked up where she left off as if there'd never been an interruption.

"So the photos never ended up in any publication as far as Kenny could tell. And she was pretty confident that she couldn't even be recognized. She said she wore a blonde wig and heavy makeup.

"But a couple of years ago, right around the time there was a big cover story on the foundation in the *Times*, she got an anonymous letter in the mail. It demanded money and included one of the photos from the session."

"Did she tell Jeremy about it?" Keri asked.

"Absolutely not. She was mortified. And she didn't want Jeremy to think ill of her. I told her that he would understand. She was twenty-three, for heaven's sake. But she wouldn't hear of it. She said that he'd be really hurt. I suggested she go to the police but she worried that would guarantee it would become public knowledge."

"She's probably right," Keri sighed.

"It was a predicament. She obviously knew who it was from so she went over to try to talk to the guy. He was still living in the same sleazy apartment that he used as his photography studio all those years ago. Kenny said he had head shots of young women plastered all over the place.

"Anyway, you can imagine how receptive he was to just dropping the whole thing. He demanded five thousand dollars a month to stay quiet. She told him that anything more than two thousand would draw her husband's attention and if he found out, the guy wouldn't have anything to blackmail her with anymore. That made sense to him and that's where they left it, Kendra paying this guy two grand every month for the last two years—until last month."

"What happened then?"

"He demanded she pay more. She said she was finally going to put an end to it."

"When was she going to do that?"

"This last weekend."

"And you don't know what happened after that?"

"I haven't talked to her since last Friday. I was surprised she didn't call but figured she'd reach out when she was ready. I'm starting to regret that."

"You couldn't have known. I get that you're worried but don't start obsessing over every potential mistake you've made."

That's my job.

Mags nodded, without a clever response for the first time that night.

What this guy's name?" Keri asked.

"Rafe Courtenay. He lives in a walk-up in Hollywood."

The waiter returned with Mags's drink and Keri's Advil, which she downed right away.

"I've got to go, Mags," she said, putting her shoes back on and dropping a ten-dollar bill on the table. "Thanks for all the info. I'll be in touch."

She had already made her way halfway across the room when she heard Mags's genteel voice behind her call out, "It was a pleasure to make your acquaintance."

She waved over her shoulder without looking back. She'd spent enough time with the Beverly Hills elite.

It was time to get down and dirty with a Hollywood sleazebag.

CHAPTER ELEVEN

Her body coursing with adrenaline, Keri pulled up in the alley behind Rafe Courtenay's apartment and sat there for a moment, preparing for what was to come. She looked at her watch.

It was almost 8:30 and the late September summer sun had set almost two hours ago. Hollywood was now lit by streetlights and the endless array of neon signs that dotted its primary boulevards.

The drive over from the Peninsula had been a busy one, with multiple phone calls. First she'd let Brody know she had to leave to follow up a lead. He was pissed until she said she was going to try to get Detectives Sterling and Cantwell sent over to help with interviews at the gala. They were almost as crusty as Brody himself and his complaining stopped at the news.

Then she called Manny Suarez to see if there was any new info from the Palm Springs bus station. There wasn't. But he did give her a rundown on Courtenay.

The guy was forty-eight, with a record of misdemeanors, most related to either DUIs or contributing to the delinquency of a minor for buying drinks for underage girls. There was nothing about blackmail and he'd never served more than a couple of days in jail.

He didn't strike Keri as an imminent threat but in her diminished physical state, threat was a relative term. And since she'd promised Mags to keep the situation off the radar if at all possible, she was reluctant to call for support, which required approval and ultimately, paperwork. That meant this had to be a solo trip. So to be safe, she changed right there in the alley.

She got out of her evening gown, strapped the rib padding back on, and followed that up with her bulletproof vest. Then she put on the hooded sweatshirt and mom jeans she'd originally planned to change into the minute she left the gala but hadn't had time to until now. Lastly she put on her sneakers, tied her hair back in the old, reliable ponytail, and strapped her police radio, Taser, handcuffs, holster, and weapon to her waistband.

The rear entrance to Courtenay's complex was locked so she made her way around front. The building was in the middle of a long block on Afton Place, a seedy side street between North Gower and Vine. As she walked, Keri recalled her last and most unpleasant phone conversation on the drive over. It was with Lieutenant Hillman.

"Why the hell did it take you so long to reach out?" he had demanded before she could get a word in. "I've talked to Brody three times today and this is the first I've heard from you since you left my office this morning."

"Sorry, sir. I've just been running around so much that I forgot to call. I guess I'm out of practice, not having been in the field for two weeks." She hated being deferential or apologetic, especially to Hillman. But she had to calm him down if she was going get him to approve her request.

"That's exactly why you need to check in more often, Locke. It's not just protocol. It's for your safety and my peace of mind."

"You're right, sir—won't happen again."

There was a brief pause in which Keri knew she'd laid it on too thick.

"What are you after, Detective? You've never been this accommodating with me, not even on your first day. You'd better come clean fast."

"It's nothing, sir. I just had a request I was hoping you could approve."

"What is it?" Hillman growled.

"I had to leave the gala to check out a time-sensitive lead and I was hoping you could send Detectives Sterling and Cantwell over there to help Brody with interviews. They seem to work well together and there are a lot of potential leads there, too many for just one person to handle."

"Sterling and Cantwell are off for the night," he said curtly.

"Yes sir. But this is a pretty high-profile case and I thought you'd want to direct all available resources to it. But I understand if that's not possible. If you prefer, we could call Beverly Hills PD and ask them to pick up the slack for us. It is, after all, their jurisdiction."

"So help me God, Locke, I hope your attempts to manipulate witnesses and suspects aren't as clunky as your attempts to manipulate me. Do you think I can't see through this—trying to make me view this as a turf war—hoping I'll protect my territory?"

"Of course not, sir," Keri answered, keeping her voice even.

"What is this lead that's so important that you had to abandon the gala, anyway?"

"It's probably nothing, sir. I don't want to waste your time with it. It'll take a half hour and then I'm on to the next thing."

"By 'the next thing,' I assume you mean following up on the Palm Springs bus station, where there seems to be actual evidence that suggests what may have actually happened, namely a rich woman bailing on her stifling life."

"That's exactly what I was going to pursue next, sir."

"Remember, Locke, there's nothing illegal about a person just dropping out of their life. If she doesn't have debts to pay or children to support, Kendra Burlingame is allowed to just disappear. And unless we can find evidence of a crime, there's no case. And if there's no case, we need to put our resources elsewhere. Do you understand?"

"Yes sir, I do. And I will keep that front of mind. But I'm almost to my destination, Lieutenant. Shall I call our Beverly Hills colleagues to help with the gala interviews or would you prefer to handle that?"

"Locke, you are a pain in my ass. I'll send our people over. Do *not* call BHPD. Finish whatever it is you're doing that you won't tell me about fast and move on. Got it?"

"Got it, sir."

Keri thought the conversation had gone about as well as it could, all things considered.

She arrived at the front entrance of Courtenay's building and studied it. It was a five-story walk-up, easily half a century old. Someone had made a sad little attempt to give it a Spanish stucco look by attaching brown tiles that had mostly cracked or broken off.

Keri stepped into the interior entry. Courtenay supposedly lived on the fourth floor in unit 412. On the resident directory, that unit was listed as "The Dream Factory." Keri felt the slight urge to vomit.

She buzzed the building manager's unit and after a minute, she was met by an elderly woman in a nightgown with her hair in rollers. Keri flashed her badge and the woman let her in.

"Are you here for the druggies in two seventeen or the pervert in four twelve?" she asked in a raspy voice.

"The pervert, ma'am," Keri answered. "But as long as we're chatting, are the druggies users or sellers?"

"Mostly users. They sell to their friends, I think."

"I can't do anything about them right now, but I can have someone come back later to deal with them if you like."

"No, that's all right. They're loud and they smell bad. But they pay their rent on time. These days, that makes for a good tenant."

"Yes, ma'am. Well, here's my card anyway. If you change your mind about that, give me a call and I'll see what I can do, okay?"

"Thank you, dear. You're not like the asshole cops I usually deal with."

"No ma'am," Keri said and started for the stairs, before turning back. "Oh, and ma'am, if you get any complaints about noise in unit four twelve, I wouldn't worry about it. Sometimes these visits can get a little rough and tumble."

The woman stared at her for a few seconds before breaking out in a wheezy cackle.

"You are a pistol, aren't you?" she laughed.

"Yes, ma'am."

"Don't worry, Detective. I'm quite hard of hearing." She cackled again and headed back to her room.

Keri began the four-story slog up to Courtenay's place. The Advil from the hotel bar was already starting to wear off and she could feel the sharp pain returning to her ribs with each step she took up the stairs. She cradled her left elbow in her right palm and pressed it against her chest to diminish the jostling.

When she reached the fourth floor, she snapped into professional mode, releasing her left arm and using her right hand to unbutton her holster. The hallway was mostly quiet, save for a few loud conversations and the noise of several televisions. Not unexpected on a Tuesday night.

She reached Courtenay's door and pressed her ear to it, hoping for some clue as to what was happening inside. But other than the muffled sound of music in the background, there was nothing. She stepped back, knocked loudly on the door, and moved to the right so that she would be out of view of the peephole and out of the direct line of fire if he reacted with gunfire instead of a hello.

She heard the music stop, followed by some rustling and the creak of floorboards.

"Who is it?" Courtenay called out from the other side of the door after about ten seconds. His voice was low and throaty.

"Detective Keri Locke, LAPD," she said as she held her badge out in front of the peephole. "I need to ask you a few questions, Mr. Courtenay."

"What about?" he demanded warily.

"Open up and I'll explain. I'm not going to shout back and forth through the door."

"You need a warrant for that," he said stubbornly.

"I need a warrant to search your place, Mr. Courtenay, not to ask you questions. Now, I came all the way over here from the West Side to chat with you. It was a long drive and I'm in a bad mood. If you want to be difficult, I can call for backup, have this door smashed open, which you'll have to pay to repair, and question you on the street in cuffs or back at my station house. That's one possible outcome. Or you can open your door and we can have a friendly chat. It's your choice but you have about five seconds to make it."

There was a brief pause before she heard several locks turn and the door opened halfway.

Rafe Courtenay stepped back far enough for her to see him and said, "I don't have to let you in."

Keri realized immediately that her assessment that Courtenay wasn't an imminent threat had been mistaken. He may have been forty-eight, but the man was in great shape. She guessed he was about six foot one and 210 pounds. He was wearing a too-tight white tank top and yoga pants and his muscles bulged in every direction. He had long brown hair that swept across his face, probably an attempt to mask his horribly pockmarked face.

Behind him, Keri could see a cabinet with several framed karate belts, including a black one, and photos of him in competitions. A pair of nunchucks hung from the wall.

It occurred to Keri that trying to talk her way into the apartment of a muscle-bound, karate-obsessed, blackmailing potential abductor while she was without backup and recovering from multiple serious injuries might not be the wisest course of action. But the thought only lasted a second before she pushed it away and replaced it with one she liked more.

That's just how I roll.

CHAPTER TWELVE

"You like karate?" Keri asked. It wasn't a sparkling conversation starter but she needed to move the discussion away from the doorway and stroking this guy's ego seemed like an effective way to get there.

Apparently it worked as Courtenay opened the door all the way so she could get a better look at his display.

"'Like' is one way to put it. A devoted practitioner is another." He tried to sound put out but his pride got the better of him and it leaked into his tone.

"So is black the best belt to have?" Keri asked as innocently as possible. She fleetingly thought that her attempts at impressed flirtation would work better if she was still in the black dress but shook the thought away. No interrogation was worth wriggling back into that thing.

"It is. I attained that twenty years ago but still train as if I have yet to achieve it." He had suddenly adopted the air of a wise karate master. Keri tried not to laugh.

"Pretty sweet," Keri said admiringly. "Mind if I get a closer look?"

"You may," he said after a brief moment of hesitation. "But that doesn't mean I'm consenting to any kind of search. I'm just being polite."

"Of course," Keri said, agreeing that he was being polite but silently rejecting his assertions beyond that. She stepped over the threshold and walked to the cabinet, taking in the room as casually as possible.

As Mags had mentioned, the walls were covered with headshots of young women, many of them signed. In the corner of the living room, she could see the door to another room that appeared to be Courtenay's photo studio. The kitchen counter was covered with bowls of fruit and she could see a huge blender next to one of them. She suspected Rafe was a big protein smoothie guy.

She reached the cabinet and turned her attention to it, hoping to find something there that she could use to keep her host's self-esteem levels inappropriately high.

"This picture looks recent," she said, pointing to one of the framed photos. "Do you do a lot of competitions these days?"

"That one's from four months ago. I got the silver in my age group, forty-five to forty-nine. But I'm forty-eight and the guy who got the gold had just turned forty-five the week before the event. So you know, not the fairest."

"Totally not fair," Keri agreed, before adding with as straight a face as she could muster, "It's hard to believe you're forty-eight."

"Hard work and healthy living," Rafe said. "In fact, I was about to make myself a kale, banana, and pear smoothie. You want one?"

"Is it good?" Keri asked, scrunching up her nose in a way she hoped came across as cute. Clearly this guy liked his ladies on the younger side, but she got the sense that he was happy to be fawned over by any woman he considered conquest-worthy.

"It's great. And so good for you."

Keri followed him to the kitchen and leaned against the counter across from him, pretending to listen while he blathered on about nutrients and restorative powers. As he spoke and prepped the drinks, she pondered the best way to start asking her questions. She'd loosened him up, but was pretty sure he'd shut down if she just dived right in.

He handed her the smoothie and she took a sip, nodding appreciatively. It wasn't the worst thing in the world but it wouldn't be replacing her bottle of Glenlivet any time soon. As Rafe chugged his drink, Keri decided she couldn't stall any longer.

"So Rafe—is it okay if I call you Rafe?" She pressed on without getting permission. "Anyway Rafe—and you should feel free to call me Keri—remember I said I had a few questions for you? I feel kind of bad about it now and about how hard I came at you when I first knocked on the door. You never know what kind of guy you're dealing with, right?"

Rafe nodded.

"Some guys are real dicks," he said.

"Exactly. So I didn't know if you were a dick too. But obviously you're not. And I feel like I can ask you these questions I have in a more casual way, you know, not so adversarial. Most of it is pretty basic stuff. And then you can get back to your evening—no harm, no foul. How does that sound?"

"It sounds okay. But I'm still not going to answer anything I'm not comfortable with. And I'm still not giving you permission to search my place without a warrant, okay?"

"Rafe, you're so silly with all the search warrant stuff. You should have been on *Law & Order* or something. You'd be very commanding as the wronged suspect, you know—the tough guy who seems guilty but is really a softie at heart. People ever tell you you're that type?"

"I've heard it from time to time."

"Speaking of acting, I know you're a photographer and it looks like you have a lot of experiences with actresses. You must be pretty good because it looks like a lot of them signed their photos. They must be happy with your work."

"I don't get a lot of complaints."

"No?" Keri asked, letting the question hang in the air.

Rafe looked at her, not sure if that was a serious question or just conversation. He said nothing. Keri placed her smoothie cup on the counter between them.

"Because here's the thing, Rafe—I know of at least one complaint. It was from a woman named Kendra Burlingame. Ever hear of her?"

Rafe put down his cup as well and waited several seconds before responding.

"If you're here, you obviously know I have. What is she complaining about?"

"Well, she hasn't filed a formal police complaint yet, if that's what you're worried about. But she has complained to friends. I think you know what about."

"So if she hasn't filed an official complaint, why are you here?"

"I'm here because she's missing, Rafe. She's been missing for over a day and a half. And I have it on good authority that you were one of the last people she spoke to before she disappeared. So I figured I'd come by and, you know, see what's up with that."

"Kendra's missing?" he asked. Keri couldn't tell if he was actually surprised or just stalling for time. In either case, she double checked that the clasp on her holster was free and that her Taser was loose too.

"She is. What did you two discuss when she came by this weekend?"

"She didn't come by," he said defiantly. She could tell he was getting agitated.

"You weren't supposed to meet with her this weekend?"

"I was. She was going to come by on Sunday afternoon. But she called at the last minute and said her sister would be coming instead."

"Did she say why?"

"No. She was super vague. I told her I didn't like dealing with anyone but her but I could tell she wasn't going to budge."

"Was this the first time anyone other than Kendra had been involved in…your arrangement?"

"Yeah. I never dealt with anyone but her this whole time."

"So her sister came over on Sunday afternoon?"

"Yeah, around four or five. I think her name is Catherine. She knocked on the door. I opened it. She handed me the envelope. I took it and closed the door. We never even spoke."

"And where were you yesterday, Rafe?"

"I was here almost all day. I had a bunch of shoots."

"I'm going to need the names and numbers of all your…clients from yesterday, to verify your alibi."

"That's not a problem."

"Good. While you're writing those down. I'm going to take a little look around. It's not an official search, just a walkabout. If what you're telling me is true, you shouldn't have any problem with that."

Rafe looked reluctant so Keri continued before he could respond.

"Rafe, honey. We both know the deal you had with Kendra. If I wanted to take you in for that, I could do it right now. But I haven't. I'm not interested in that. I'm interested in finding Kendra Burlingame. Unless there's something you have in this apartment that suggests you were in involved in her disappearance, I'm going to overlook anything I find. This is a good deal for you."

Rafe seemed to see the logic of her words and nodded. While he wrote down the girls he'd photographed the day before, Keri checked out the rest of his place, starting with the bedroom he'd converted into his studio. She moved on to his bedroom and the bathroom, then the hall closet. She looked up every few seconds to make sure Rafe was still seated at the kitchen counter.

The place wasn't very big and the whole search took less than ten minutes. She found nothing—no blood, no sign of struggle, no secret torture chamber. It was just the bachelor apartment of a sleazy, over-the-hill photographer who engaged in a little blackmail on the side. Keri doubted Kendra was his only victim. She returned to the kitchen, where Rafe was waiting with the completed list of names.

"Thanks, sweetie," she said as she pocketed it. "There's just one more thing I need from you."

"What's that?" he asked.

"The pictures of Kendra—all of them, including the negatives."

"What?" His face dropped.

"Every picture you ever took of Kendra and every negative. I need them—now. I'm sure you've got all of them in some precious file somewhere. So please hand it over."

"I can't do that."

"Why not?"

"Because I can—they're my prop—I just won't."

"Sure you will, Rafe. You see, I'm not going to just leave them here and let you potentially destroy evidence of your connection to someone who's been abducted. If it turns out your alibi is bullshit, I'll need them to prosecute you."

"But you need a warrant…" he said less confidently than he had the first time.

"We're back to that again? Nothing's changed, Rafe. I can still get that warrant. I can still haul you back to the station. The only way you stay in this apartment tonight is if you give me Kendra's complete file right now."

Rafe seemed to be weighing his options. At a certain point, she saw something click for him. She didn't like it. His body, which had been tense, appeared to relax a bit.

"I've been wondering why you keep asking me to give you the stuff and didn't just come here with a bunch of cops, bust down the door with a search warrant, and look for it yourself. And I think I know why."

"Why is that?" she asked.

"Because that would mean bad publicity for Kendra. And you're trying to protect her from that. You know she's been paying up for years and you don't want what she did to come out if you can avoid it. But if you come in here hard, it'll get out and be in the papers and stuff. You're a softie, Keri."

He took the tiniest step toward her. Keri felt her skin crawl and tingle at the same time.

"You're not thinking clearly, Rafe. I did it this way because getting a warrant takes a while and every second counts when you're trying to save a missing person's life. Besides, if this goes public, every girl you photograph will know what you did to Kendra. I wonder how your business will do once you're tagged as a blackmailing pornographer."

"It might improve," he said, taking another step forward.

Keri could tell talk wasn't going to work anymore. Rafe, despite her best efforts, felt trapped. And he thought he sensed weakness in her. It was a dangerous combination, especially considering that she *was* physically weaker than usual.

He was only about four feet away from her now and she could see the growing agitation in Rafe's eyes. He was no longer thinking about the consequences of what he was about to do. He felt threatened. He thought he could defeat that threat. And any second he would try.

61

"Rafe..." she started to say, hoping to deescalate the situation. But it was too late. He leapt at her in a forceful but controlled way.

He was surprisingly fast but Keri had been expecting something and stepped back quickly. Sure, her ribs and shoulder hurt like hell but her legs worked just fine. Rafe may have been a black belt in karate but Keri had extensive training in Krav Maga, and one of her favorite lessons from her instructors was to let your opponent be the aggressor and react to that aggression.

As Rafe continued to move forward, his fists striking out toward her, Keri pulled out the Taser she'd quietly removed from its holster and jabbed it hard against her attacker's left forearm. He didn't stop completely but his frenzied eyes looked confused and he glanced down to see why his arm felt so funny.

At that moment, Keri moved forward and jabbed the Taser to his neck. His body shivered involuntarily before he crumpled to the ground. Keri leaned down and jabbed him once more between the shoulder blades, just to be sure.

Rafe stopped moving. As quickly as she could, Keri holstered the Taser, pulled out her handcuffs, and secured his arms behind his back. Then she rolled him over. He offered no resistance.

When Rafe came to a few moments later, Keri was sitting a chair beside him, Taser still in hand.

"How ya feeling, Rafe?" she asked casually. "Looks like your big boy belt didn't get the job done this time."

Rafe shook his head as if he were trying to get rid of invisible cobwebs.

"Whaa...?" he muttered.

"Your brain working okay there, fella? Let me explain the situation to you. But know that I'm only going to do this once. You just attempted to assault a police officer. That was a bad choice. I mean 'forget about competing in the fifty-to-fifty-four-year-old division' bad. We're one phone call away from you finding out how much that black belt helps when you go up against Big Tiny and his crew in the prison yard.

"But I'm giving you one last literal get out of jail free card. Before, all I wanted were Kendra's photos and negatives. But now you're going to hand over the materials for every woman you've been blackmailing. I know there are others. You do that and I'll forget about what just happened."

Rafe grunted inaudibly and tried to shake his head. Keri decided he needed some added incentive.

"Otherwise," she continued, "you'll be cancelling all your photo sessions for the next five to eight years. And don't leave out even one woman. If you do, I'll find out and I'll come back to arrest you and confiscate every photo you've taken in your entire career. Your call—one time only offer. And it expires in three, two, one…"

CHAPTER THIRTEEN

With a deep sense of satisfaction, Keri locked the photos and negatives of Kendra and sixteen other women in the small file cabinet by her office desk and headed over to the tech room. She had been tempted to burn them on the drive over. But if Rafe Courtenay turned out to be Kendra's abductor, they'd be needed as evidence.

For the time being all she could do was hold on to them. That and give Rafe one last jolt before she took off the cuffs and left him lying on the floor in a pool of his own urine.

The tech room was a large, darkened office filled with computers connected to numerous city, state, and federal databases. There were multiple sizeable monitors affixed to various walls throughout the room. Detectives Edgerton and Suarez were currently staring at one with some grainy black-and-white footage.

"What are we looking at, boys?" she asked.

"We pulled up the footage from the Palm Springs bus station for you," said Manny Suarez, a short, roundish forty-something guy with three days of beard growth and sleepy eyes that hid a sharp intellect.

"I hope it's useful or I'm going to have to head out there myself," Keri said.

"Lieutenant Hillman's already grumbling that you haven't done that yet," Suarez said. "That reminds me. He wanted me to tell you he set up an interview for you with Kendra's sister, Catherine. It's at her house in West Adams tomorrow morning at eight a.m."

"Yeah, he said that if you missed it, he'd have you put back on desk duty," added Kevin Edgerton, the baby of the Pacific Division detective squad. Tall and lanky, with light brown hair that he was always brushing out of his eyes, he was only twenty-eight.

But he'd already distinguished himself with his incredible technical expertise. He had a way of navigating databases, sifting through statistical data and cracking computer information that rivaled Keri's ability to understand and predict human behavior. He was her best hope of finally cracking the code to Pachanga's laptop.

Right now, he was typing furiously away at a keyboard, clearly annoyed by something.

"What is it, Kevin?" Keri asked.

"I'm just frustrated. Look here—this is when we see Kendra's car pull into the bus station parking garage. There's her license plate in the freeze frame. It's kind of hard to see because the ticket dispenser is blocking her face, but there she is reaching for the parking ticket at the entry gate. The time is nine thirty-one a.m."

"That fits. If she left her house soon after her husband did, she could reasonably get to Palm Springs by then," Keri noted.

"Right," Suarez agreed. "Then we see her here, here, and here as she makes her way to the third level of the structure. But that's the last image we have of the car. And it's right around then, at nine thirty-six a.m., that the GPS goes off in both the car and her phone. Palm Springs police found it in one of the few spots in the garage that isn't covered by security cameras. What are the chances of that?"

"Not very high," Keri said. "Look at all the available parking spots her car passed by on the way to the third level. It was a conscious choice to park in the spot where the car ended up. The question is why."

"That's not the only question," Edgerton added. "I'm wondering where the hell she went. There's no definitive video of her leaving the garage or entering the bus station."

"Nothing at all?" Keri asked, flummoxed.

"Well, not quite nothing," said Suarez. "We used the photos you sent us of her and we found a couple of images that could be her. But we never see her clearly so we can't do facial recognition."

"Pull up your likely suspects and let's check them out," Keri said.

While Edgerton did that, Keri turned to Suarez.

"I assume you guys already pulled up cell phone records for Kendra from yesterday. Anything interesting?"

"Nope," he said. "She didn't make a single call from Beverly Hills to Palm Springs."

"What about Jeremy Burlingame?"

"His records are clean too," Suarez said, clearly disappointed. "There are several texts and missed calls from him to her today, but nothing suspicious. And nothing much at all yesterday, which makes sense considering he was in surgery most of the time."

As Keri turned that over in her head, Edgerton pulled up the surveillance clips. They showed four women entering the bus station within ten minutes of the car pulling into the garage. Keri understood why the guys thought they might all be options but she immediately dismissed two of them.

One was about five foot three and Kendra was closer to five foot ten. Another, even without seeing her face, was obviously in her early twenties. Keri couldn't have explained how she knew—

something about the taut skin and the bouncy walk told her this was not a mature woman.

It took her a second longer to dispense with the third. The height and build were right. But something was off. Finally, it hit her. The woman's hair was dark blonde. Since the footage was black and white, she didn't register the hair color consciously at first. But glancing back at a photo of Kendra and her jet black hair, she realized it couldn't be the same person.

The last woman had on sunglasses and a headscarf that reminded Keri of something Audrey Hepburn would wear while hiding herself from the press circa 1959.

She was the right height and her bearing fit with a woman in her late thirties or early forties. Her outfit—casual slacks, long gloves, and a loose, sophisticated blouse—suggested a woman going on vacation or spending a day at the country club. It felt like it could be her.

"I think that could be our gal. Don't we have video from inside the station as she enters?" she asked.

"Of course not," Manny said caustically. "Why would they want to make it easy on us? The interior camera showing the main entrance is down. It has been since last week. There are lots of other cameras inside but the place is so crowded and until now, we didn't have anyone to focus on."

"We still don't," said Edgerton. "The cameras are positioned so high up and there are so many people milling about that finding her is going to be finding a needle in, well, you get it."

"Okay. So forget that," Keri suggested. "Maybe if you try to work backward."

"What do you mean?" both men asked in unison.

"Jinx. You owe me a Coke," Edgerton said playfully.

"I'm gonna owe you a fist sandwich if you're not careful, baby boy," Suarez growled.

"Just trying to lighten the mood," Edgerton muttered under his breath.

"If you kids are done," Keri said, "I'll tell you what I mean. If we can figure out which bus she was planning to take, maybe we can ID her, or at least follow the footage back until we get a clear image. Plus, we'll know her destination—two for one."

"I knew we kept you around for a reason," Suarez joked as Edgerton looked up the bus itineraries from yesterday morning.

"Within two hours of her arrival at the bus station, there were six departures: San Francisco, Las Vegas, Denver, Phoenix, San Diego, and Los Angeles. But almost all of them continue on to

66

additional destinations. The Vegas bus eventually goes all the way New York. The Phoenix one ends up in Orlando. The San Fran bus continues on to Portland and Seattle. San Diego stops at the border with Tijuana. I mean, how do you pin that down?"

Keri was quiet. Both men knew not to interrupt when she was in that zone.

San Diego makes a little sense if she continued on to Tijuana. If she wanted to get lost, Mexico is a good place to start. But Kendra doesn't feel like a Tijuana kind of girl. No reason to come back to LA. So where?

And then it came to her so suddenly she was embarrassed it took so long.

"Check the manifest for Phoenix," she said.

Edgerton pulled it up. They all scanned it at the same time. The name Kendra Burlingame was nowhere in sight. Keri felt her spirits starting to fade when a name caught her eye.

"Click on that one, Kevin," she said, pointing to one name that felt familiar. The ticket details indicated that it was purchased with cash the day of departure. No help there.

"Why are we checking a passenger named A. Maroney?" Suarez asked.

"Because Kendra's full maiden name is Kendra Ann Maroney and she was raised in Phoenix, Arizona."

"Nice!" Edgerton exclaimed, unable to contain his youthful enthusiasm.

"So let's go to the camera showing passengers getting on the Phoenix bus and see if we have any luck," she suggested.

Edgerton pulled up the video and after a few minutes the same woman in the slacks, gloves, and blouse with the sunglasses and headscarf stepped aboard.

"Her head is down so we still can't do facial recognition," Edgerton noted.

"Yeah, it's almost like she's trying to hide her face or something," Suarez said sarcastically. "I think at this point we can safely say she didn't want folks to know she was taking this trip."

"Back it up, Kevin," Keri said, ignoring their squabbling. It was almost ten at night and the long day was clearly starting to fray their nerves. "Let's see when she enters the frame and then find out what camera might have last caught an image of her."

"Oh, I get it," he said, matching up her location at the start of the bus video with where she was in relation to the next nearest video camera. Using the process, they were able to track her location from the bus, back to a small shop in the station, where she looked around a bit before buying a snack.

Before that, they tracked her to the women's restroom. Before that she sat for a while in one of the station's general seating areas. They back timed her movements from there to the ticket window. And prior to that, she was walking down a long corridor in the main hall of the station. That's where the footage ended, which made sense, since the next logical image would have come from the broken camera facing the station entrance.

"Okay, so we have her timeline once she entered the station. How does that help us?" Edgerton asked.

"I'm not sure yet," Keri answered. "Why don't we take a step back and just watch it. Can you reverse it so we can see her movements as they actually happened?"

"Of course."

Edgerton set the video in motion and they watched it mostly in real time, except for the twenty minutes when she just read a magazine in general seating.

"Can you zoom in to see what she's reading?" Keri asked.

"I can do it after we're done with the video. It might take a few hours to render but we've got a decent shot. What will that do?"

"I don't know. I'm grasping at straws here."

They returned their attention to the screen as the woman got up and went to the ladies' room. She came out after a few minutes and went to the shop, where she looked around briefly before buying what looked like a granola bar and leaving the frame.

"Go back again to when she's looking around," Keri requested.

Edgerton replayed the video.

"Freeze it there," Keri shouted. "Are there any other camera angles in the store?"

"Let me check." Edgerton punched a few keys and another view came up from the interior of the store. When it got to the same point as the other video, he froze it. The woman had picked up a small circular tchotchke.

"What is that?" Suarez asked.

"I think it's a snow globe," Edgerton said, "and I think I can make out the lettering. It says... 'Palm Springs.' Why would there be a Palm Springs snow globe? It doesn't snow there."

"It's a dumb souvenir," Suarez said. "Who cares why they made it snow there? I'm wondering why she picked that particular one. It could be significant. What do you think, Keri?"

"Maybe, but that's not why I'm interested in it. Look, she's not wearing her gloves. I realized she wasn't wearing them when she left the bathroom. She must have taken them off in there and forgot to put them back on when she left. But she's wearing them again when she gets on the bus."

"What's the significance of that?" Edgerton asked. "So we know she practices good hygiene and washed her hands."

Keri looked down at the young detective. He was a technical genius and she hoped that his skills would help her break Pachanga's code. But sometimes he was a little dense. She tried not to sound condescending when she responded.

"The significance is that, unless someone else bought that snow globe in the last two days, we have that woman's prints."

CHAPTER FOURTEEN

Kendra felt the full weight of the day as she pulled into the Marina Bay parking lot. Her eyes were heavy and the aches and pains that had been annoying throughout the day were near overwhelming now.

There wasn't much she could do back at the station tonight. She asked Edgerton to contact Palm Springs PD to see if they could get prints off the snow globe, assuming it was still there. Suarez volunteered to get in touch with Phoenix police to try to secure video from the bus station there. The hope was to track Kendra's movements from there to whatever her next destination was in that city.

But both of those things would take until morning at least. Keri decided to take advantage of the lull to go home, clean up, and maybe get a little sleep.

But as she trudged toward the twenty-year-old houseboat that had been her home for the last few years, she couldn't stop her mind from racing through the details of the case. Why would Kendra just up and leave her life? Why did no one she knew—her husband, her friends Mags and Becky Sampson, even that scumbag Rafe—think she was capable of that? And yet, the evidence so far suggested that she had.

I'm missing something. I'm looking at this wrong somehow.

But she couldn't figure out how to change her perspective. The frustration was making her antsy.

Keri reached her boat and stepped aboard. Maybe taking a mental break would help.

Sea Cups was essentially a ramshackle floating shed. It had been named by a guy who clearly wasn't a proud feminist and Keri had never bothered to change it or paint it over. It had the basics—a bed, a galley, a small living space, and a stairwell that led to a second level with a chaise lounge chair and a rusty metal card table. It was a pretty bare-bones operation. Showering and laundry required trips to the marina's comfort station, a quarter-mile walk away.

Keri had grown weary of the lifestyle and while in the hospital, she had decided to do some apartment hunting once she was more fully healed. She and Ray had even traded newspapers, circling places in the classifieds that might fit the bill. The friendly nurses would shuttle between their rooms, handing them off to each other.

It was a way to pass the time when they were both stuck in hospital beds.

But she was serious about making the move. Despite the cost, she planned to stay in the area, even if meant getting something tiny. But she wanted a place with two bedrooms. That was the key. It was her way of maintaining hope that she would eventually find Evie and bring her home, wherever home might be.

Keri didn't have the energy to trek to the comfort station so she splashed some water on her face and called it a shower. She kicked off her sneakers and opened the fridge. There was almost nothing there. She improvised, scrambling up some eggs and tossing them in a tortilla. Then she sat down at the tiny galley table and scarfed them down in less than a minute.

She thought about going up on deck to decompress but there was a cool wind blowing through the marina and she wasn't in the mood to brave it. Instead, she plopped down on the couch, opened a half-empty bottle of Glenlivet, and allowed herself a healthy pour.

Then she reached under the table and pulled out a shoebox filled with blank index cards and different colored Sharpies. She wrote down the names of everyone connected to the case and their affiliation to Kendra, then spread them out on the table and stared, waiting for inspiration to strike. None did.

She took a long sip of her drink and let her eyes wander to the corner of the room, where a half dozen unopened packing boxes rested against a wall. She had bought them her first day out of the hospital and planned to begin packing stuff up right away.

But then the realization that she ought to have an apartment locked in first hit her. And besides, every time she looked at the photos she was supposed to be packing up, her memories overwhelmed her.

She took another sip, closed her eyes, and let the scotch fill her insides with its warm burn. Images swam through her head.

She saw the blue September sky, the bright green grass of the park where she and Evie had been sitting almost exactly five years ago. She saw her eight-year-old daughter's wide smile with its chipped upper tooth, her pig-tailed blonde hair, her lacy white socks, and hot pink tennis shoes.

She saw the back of the man running away with Evie, across the broad green expanse of the park and into the parking lot, where he tossed her roughly into a white van. She saw the man stab a teenage boy who ran to help. She saw a wisp of blond hair under the man's cap and part of a tattoo on the right side of his neck before he disappeared into the van and tore off. She saw that the van had no license plates. She felt the sharp gravel digging into her bare feet as she ran across the parking lot, trying to catch up to the van speeding away with her beloved daughter inside.

She saw it all. Then she opened her eyes, wet with tears, finished the last of her drink, and stood up. Her night wasn't over just yet.

*

In the car on the way to Jackson Cave's office, Keri, hyped up on anticipation and anxiety, looked at herself in the rearview mirror and sighed.

It's a good thing I'm not planning to charm my way in there because this look isn't going to win anyone over.

Keri hadn't bothered to change. For what she had in mind, staying in her hooded sweatshirt and mom jeans might be preferable.

As she changed freeways from the 405 north to the 10 east, doubt crept into her mind.

Is this really the smartest move right now? Am I putting my entire career in jeopardy?

As she so often did when faced with a dilemma of this kind, Keri decided to ignore the current awkwardness between them and called Ray.

"Hello…?" said a sleepy voice on the other end of the line. Keri glanced at the clock in her car.

Damn, it's eleven forty-five at night. He was sleeping. The guy is recovering from a gunshot wound, after all.

"Ray? Sorry. I forgot what time it was. I'll call you tomorrow."

"What's up?" he asked a little less groggily.

"I wanted your opinion on something, but it can wait until tomorrow," she lied.

"I'm up now. You may as well ask."

That was all the opening she needed.

"So I think I may be making a really terrible professional decision right now."

"Okay," Ray said. "Well, now I'm completely awake—go on."

"I'm driving downtown right now to break into Jackson Cave's law office."

There was a long pause.

"Well, it's a good thing I'm in the hospital," Ray said finally.

"Why?"

"Because the doctors won't have far to go to treat my heart attack. Are you friggin' crazy, Keri?"

"I have been accused."

"Turn your car around right now."

"So I take it you think this *is* a terrible professional decision?"

"I think it's not just a terrible professional decision. It's one that could get you locked up. Why do you want to do this?"

"Edgerton and I have hit a wall with Pachanga's computer. We need the right cipher to break the code. Otherwise, it's useless. So I visited Cave this afternoon, to see what I could learn and try to rattle him."

"Did you?"

"I'm not sure. Maybe a little bit. I have a hunch about something."

"About what?" Ray asked.

"I don't want to say. I don't want you to get in trouble."

"You tell me you're planning to bust into the workplace of an officer of the court and *now* you're going to play coy to protect me? It's a little late for that, don't you think, Mini-Me?"

"Listen, Optimus Prime—if I'm arrested, you can always say you told me not to go and I changed my mind based on that. In fact, at the end of this conversation, I'll do just that. And you're all drugged up so you'll believe me and go right back to sleep. But if I give more specifics, you might really be in a pickle if you're called as a witness."

"You are the craziest chick I have ever met in my life," Ray said.

Keri couldn't tell if he was horrified or impressed.

"Thank you?" she replied.

"You do realize that if you're caught, you are playing into the hands of the very man who may know the truth about Evie's disappearance. Do you really want to give this guy that kind of power?"

"I don't have a choice, Ray. I feel like I have to do something bold. It's been five years since she was taken. This is the best lead I've gotten. I can't just sit on it. I can't."

"I know."

They both fell silent. Keri kept her watery eyes on the freeway, imagining Ray lying in his hospital bed, picturing his strong hand holding the phone to his ear.

"What's going on with the other case?" he finally asked. "The one with the missing wife."

"Oh, that. We're still working it. Not sure what to make of it yet. Maybe I'll give you call in a few hours to pick your brain on that one. How does three a.m. sound?"

"It sounds good, assuming you're not in jail."

"Why would I be in jail, Ray? After all, I'm following your professional advice. I'm turning around to go back home. I have decided not to pursue my crazy plan."

"You're very convincing. I totally believe you," Ray said, unconvinced and disbelieving.

"Good night, Ray."

"Good night, Keri. And good luck."

Keri hung up and continued on her chosen route. She could see the tower in the distance but wasn't headed there quite yet.

She had to make one brief pit stop on the way.

CHAPTER FIFTEEN

Keri tried not to let her nervousness show as she stood in the US Bank Tower security office, watching the night security manager review her fake ID.

For a manager, he looked awfully young. He was gangly and his uniform hung loosely on his skeletal frame. Despite his apparent inexperience, he seemed dubious about her claim for being here. But since she was already officially breaking the law, she decided to go all in.

"How long are you going to look at that thing, Mr. Delacruz? You're starting to make me wonder if it's not just the janitorial staff I should be investigating."

"I'm sorry, Officer Bird," he said, handing her back the ID. "It's just that no one informed me there was even an investigation of the cleaning company, much less that you would be doing a sting operation."

"First of all, that's what a sting is, Mr. Delacruz. If we informed you ahead of time, it would kind of defeat the purpose. Second, it's Detective Sue Bird, not officer. I worked hard for the promotion and I'd appreciate the respect I've earned."

Sue Bird was actually the name of a real woman's professional basketball player. Keri had chosen her name for her fake cop ID because Bird was tough and hard-nosed. It helped her stay in character.

"Of course," Delacruz said, flustered and no longer on the offensive. "What is it you need again exactly?"

"I need a janitorial uniform and access keys to the all the interior offices on the sixty-ninth, seventieth, and seventy-first floors. That's where we believe the suspect will be this evening."

"And you really think one of the crew is stealing things from the offices?"

"We know that a private firm is paying janitorial staff from a cleaning company to copy private material from computers in various high-profile businesses in the downtown area. We've narrowed it down to two cleaning companies. The one you use is one of them. We have another sting going on right now in a different downtown building for the other company. Our hope is that we can close this case tonight."

"I really think I should call the day security manager to get permission, Detective Bird."

"You're free to do that. But I should warn you that if it turns out that the company cleaning this building is the culprit, prosecutors might consider your attempts to interfere in the sting as collusion with the criminals and you might face charges of conspiracy to commit theft. But it's your call, of course, Mr. Delacruz."

The man only needed a second to make his decision before deciding to skip the call and lead her to the women's janitorial locker room.

As Keri followed him, she allowed herself a silent sigh of relief. She'd never used her fake ID and was beginning to wonder if Ray had been kidding when he'd suggested she get one "just in case" a year ago. He had said that sometimes it was helpful to be a cop other than yourself. She hadn't really understood what he meant at the time but she did now.

"Here you go, Detective. Uniforms are over there. You can pick the size that best fits you. I'll be back in a couple of minutes with the keys."

When he left, Keri changed as quickly as she could out of her sweatshirt and jeans. It took longer than she liked because of the shoulder and rib injuries, but she took care not to visibly wince or give any hint that she was in pain.

Who knows if there are cameras in the locker room? Can't leave any bread crumbs.

She took off the cap she'd been wearing low over her eyes, making sure not to remove the disheveled brown-haired wig she had on. She changed into a bulky janitorial uniform to hide her build and stuffed a pair of latex gloves into the pants pocket.

Even if there were none in the locker room, the rest of the building was covered in security cameras and there was no way Keri could locate all of them. So her best bet was to keep her face hidden and leave no prints. Even if she got away with this, the security staff, Cave himself, and possibly the police would be reviewing every second of footage they could find to uncover who Detective Sue Bird really was. Any mistake and she'd be found out, arrested, and likely incarcerated.

That's why she had parked twelve blocks away, in an outdoor lot without cameras, walked to a Metro station, and ridden the train to the stop near the tower. It's why she was wearing an old pair of black loafers she hadn't put on in months and would toss after tonight so no shoeprints could be traced to her. It's why she wore a pair of fake tinted eyeglasses. And it's why she had been using a pretty lame southern accent while talking to Delacruz.

He knocked on the door. Keri gave herself one last once-over and, satisfied that she couldn't easily be identified as herself, stepped outside to begin the next phase of her plan.

*

Keri got out of the service elevator on the seventieth floor and made her way to the door with the tube latch hole she'd stuffed the tissue into. Pretending to use the key card Mr. Delacruz had given her, she pushed on the door. It gave way and she was able to open it.

She stepped inside and readjusted the latex gloves she'd put on as she'd entered the elevator on the lobby level. She stood there silently, trying to think. Getting a key card instead of actual metal keys had messed with her plan. She'd been lucky that the tissue worked on the exterior door. But any office she opened from this point on would register on the building's security system with a timestamp, location, and user ID.

Of course in this case, the card would register as being an all-purpose guest or staff card. But when they checked later, it wouldn't be hard to back trace the user to the non-existent detective who had showed up in the middle of the night.

That meant that eventually Jackson Cave would know that someone other than the normal cleaning staff had entered his personal office. When he made that discovery, he'd surely move the cipher or even destroy it. So she only had this one chance to find it.

As she walked quickly down the hall toward his office, she had an idea.

I don't have to just open Cave's office. I can open them all and hide my true target.

Cave's office was in the corner of the building so Keri began at one end of the long hallway, methodically unlocking each attorney's door. After she opened Cave's, she continued on down the other hallway until they were all open.

Even though she couldn't see them, Keri knew there were cameras everywhere, so she went into several offices, pretending to look around, hoping her movements would throw them off her scent when they watched her later.

When she got to Cave's office, Keri knew exactly where to go but held back for a second. A guy like Jackson Cave would certainly have additional security beyond whatever the building offered.

He likely had several electronic tripwires that would warn him if someone breached his files, his computer, or anything else he thought important. It was entirely possible that he'd call Delacruz the second one went off. Or worse, that he'd head straight to the office.

It occurred to Keri that she had no idea where Cave lived.

Downtown has become a hip residential area recently. What if he's got a penthouse apartment somewhere nearby? He could be here in minutes.

It was too late to do anything about that now, so she stepped in and walked straight to the photo of Cave with the monsignor. When she'd commented on it during her earlier visit that afternoon, he had tensed up ever so imperceptibly. If the cipher was anywhere in his office, it was near that picture.

She lifted it off the wall and felt the slightest hint of resistance, and then it came free. Glancing at the wall behind the frame, she saw a thin electrical wire hanging down. It had obviously been connected to the back of the frame. The connection had been severed, which was almost certainly the trigger she'd been afraid Cave might have.

Oh well, at least I'm on the right track.

Keri glanced at her watch. It was 12:32 a.m. She imagined she had ten minutes tops to get out of the building if Cave was calling security. She pulled his chair out and sat down under his desk where no cameras could see what she was doing.

Then she felt around the frame's fabric backing until her gloved fingers ran over a small bump the size of a flash drive. She peeled away the backing and pulled out the drive. After that she fished out the old Android phone she'd brought, connected it to the drive with a USB OTG cable, and started the download.

There was only one file on the drive and the whole process took less than a minute. Keri shoved the phone and cable back in her pocket, replaced the flash drive behind the frame, and started to put it back on the wall.

But realizing there was no point to that now, she tried another tack. Instead of replacing the photo, she dropped it on the ground, letting the glass shatter. Then she removed and dropped several other photos along that wall. Maybe she could convince Cave that the frames had fallen off the wall in a minor earthquake. It wasn't a solution, but it might hold him off until he saw the video footage.

Keri ran down the hall as fast as her battered body would allow and rushed out the same side door she had entered the office through. She hurried to the service elevator and hit the down button.

The doors opened immediately. She considered that a good sign. If it wasn't there, it probably meant that Delacruz or one of his men was on the way up.

She rode down, making sure to keep her head tilted downward and her cap low, continually checking her watch. 12:37 a.m. It was hard to imagine that Cave hadn't gotten hold of Delacruz or another security guard by now. She wouldn't be surprised if they were waiting for her in the lobby right now.

Keri looked up. She was on the fourth floor and moving fast. She reached out and hit the button for the second floor hard. The elevator stopped a moment later and she stepped out. She was halfway down the hall by the time she heard the ding indicating that the doors were closing again.

She got to the door for the stairs at the end of the hall and peeked through the small window. No one was there. She opened the door and made her way down to the lobby. There was no window on that door so she opened it slightly and peeked out. She couldn't see anyone but she could hear loud voices.

"Report to me as soon as you have her," she heard Delacruz ordering someone. She stepped out and moved quietly down the hall. A loud ding told her a guard had likely just gotten in the service elevator and was headed up to look for her. There was another security guard at the front desk with his back to her.

She rounded the corner in time to see Delacruz returning to the security office, likely to inform Cave on their progress in finding her. Once the door closed, she tiptoed down the hall back to the janitorial changing room. She didn't have time to put on her clothes but she didn't want to leave them there either. Delacruz would eventually remember they were there and someone would think to pull DNA off them.

She stuffed them in a trash bag, threw it over her shoulder, and left through the employee back door that allowed them to enter and exit the building without fancy suited people having to lay eyes on them.

The door led down a long hallway, which came to a narrow stairwell. She took it down and opened the door at the bottom. It opened into an underground parking garage that seemed to go on for miles.

Keri saw a security booth at the far end and walked the other way, toward a door that looked to be a pedestrian exit. She opened it and found that it was actually a long tunnel that elevated slowly. She followed it until it came to another door that opened at street level.

She stepped outside and took a deep breath. She was finally out of the tower complex. But she was far from safe yet.

CHAPTER SIXTEEN

With her blood pumping hard, Keri crouched uncomfortably in the corner of the small parking lot, desperately sucking in air and ignoring the pain in her throbbing ribs. She had run here when she heard the nearby sirens and barely made it behind the lot's four-foot-high concrete wall before a squad car tore around the corner.

She waited for the sound to fade before standing up again. She was two blocks away from the tower now, still dangerously close. She was over ten blocks away from her car and there was no way she could return the way she'd come, by Metro. It would be crawling with police looking for a woman in a janitorial uniform.

She had to find somewhere with people, somewhere crowded where she could change and then blend into the crowd so she could get away unnoticed. She hurried northwest up South Grand Avenue in the direction of her car, keeping her eyes open for someplace to duck in.

The sound of loud, pulsing house music emanated from somewhere on West 4th and she cut over that way. Near the corner of South Olive, she saw a club called The Gentry. A long line out front snaked around the corner. There was no way the bouncer would let her in the way she was dressed so she ducked into an alley behind the building.

As she reached the back door of the club, she heard more sirens very close by. She banged on the door loudly and waited, hoping someone would open it before floodlights from an LAPD squad car illuminated the alley.

After what seemed like an eternity, the door opened. A petite woman in her fifties wearing a hairnet and apron stood in front of her. The woman looked Keri up and down, then started to shut the door.

Keri put her foot in the gap to block it and pleaded.

"Please let me in."

The woman seemed ready to force the door closed when she caught the sound of the nearby sirens. Her eyes widened and she peeked around the door to see if they were visible. The red and blue lights weren't in sight yet but they sounded like they couldn't be more than a block away.

"*Policia?*" she asked in a hushed, fearful voice.

"*Sí,*" Keri whispered back.

The woman stared at her for another endless moment. Then, without a word, she pulled her inside.

"Thank you," Keri whispered.

"*Sigueme*," the woman said, beckoning for Keri to follow her. She led the way down a small hallway to what appeared to be an employee changing room.

"Thanks," Keri repeated, sitting down on the tiny bench in the middle of the small room.

"*Aspera aquí*," the woman said, holding up her hand. Keri's Spanish was limited but she got the gist. The woman wanted her to stay in the room.

When she left, Keri proceeded to change out of the cleaning uniform and back into the sweatshirt and jeans from before. About halfway through the slow, laborious process, the woman returned. She was holding clothes, which she immediately hung up on the back of the door.

Keri was surprised at what she saw. The woman had secured a loose navy skirt, a lavender tank top, and a pair of stylish black flats. She also had a black beret and a small change purse, just large enough for Keri's fake ID and the Android phone with the data from Cave's flash drive.

"Where did you get all this?" Keri asked, stunned.

"Lost and Found," the woman replied in a thick accent. Then without asking, the woman came over and took the shaggy brunette wig off Keri's head, pulled a hair tie from her pocket, and put her hair up into a tight bun. She stepped back and nodded approvingly.

Over the next few minutes, the woman helped her into the outfit and adjusted the beret so that none of Keri's blonde hair was visible. The woman took the cleaning uniform, Keri's clothes, and the cap and stuffed them all in a plastic bag.

"*Quemar*," she said as she pulled out a lighter. Apparently she was going to burn Keri's stuff.

"I can't thank you enough. What's your name?"

"Esmerelda," the woman said, smiling. She pointedly didn't ask for Keri's name and Keri didn't offer it.

"What now?"

"*Ven*," Esmerelda said, beckoning for Keri to follow her. They made their way through the back of the club, past the dishwashers and the cooks, all of whom pointedly kept their heads down as she walked by.

When they reached the door leading from the kitchen to the club itself, Esmerelda pointed through the window in the direction of the club entrance. Keri nodded her understanding.

"*Gracias*," she said.

Esmerelda nodded and opened the door for her without a word. Keri stepped through and made her way to the front of the club with her head down, sliding by the dancing patrons and the rowdy drinkers, trying to be as unobtrusive as possible.

When she got outside she was on Olive and followed it north all the way back to the parking lot. There were still occasional sirens but they all seemed to be centered near the tower. She hadn't seen a single police vehicle on her walk back.

Her car was still there, sitting lonely in the mostly empty lot. The cardboard she had taped to her front and rear license plates was still in place. She got in and drove off, following every traffic law to the letter, taking surface streets instead of the freeway until she made it to a residential street.

She was in the West Adams District, the same neighborhood where Kendra Burlingame's sister, Catherine, lived. Everything was quiet. Keri could feel her heart rate slowly returning to normal.

She pulled out the phone and turned it on. Waiting for the information to load, Keri tried to keep her expectations in check. It was possible that this file could contain everything she'd need to help her find Evie. Or it could be just another dead end.

It turned out to be something in between. When the screen loaded, Keri saw that she needed to input a password to access the cipher. The fact that whatever was on the drive was password protected *and* had been hidden behind a picture frame suggested that it was the real deal. But she had no clue how to begin to uncover what Cave's password was.

Damn it! How am I going to break this password?

Part of her considered just staying here and trying options until she cracked it. But she knew that was almost certainly a waste of time. Besides, she was exhausted and might make some kind of irreparable mistake. As infuriating as it was, she needed to look at it again when she had fresh eyes.

She briefly considered easing her seat back and crashing here until her interview with Catherine in the morning. But that would mess up the alibi she'd so meticulously planned out. So she shook the thought from her head and continued to her next destination.

*

Keri lay on the massage table. Her eyes were droopy with exhaustion but she tried to force herself not to fall asleep. Her goal was made a little easier by the masseuse, who was giving her a fairly intense body scrub. She had tried to explain to the woman to steer clear of her ribs and shoulder but she was still occasionally jarred by an overly firm swipe. As she tried to relax, Keri reviewed her situation.

Her alibi was in place and she thought it would hold. Before going to Cave's office, she'd stopped in Koreatown to book a massage in one of their all-night spas. These places were some of LA's oddest but increasingly popular hangouts. Many of them were open 24/7 and offered everything from rubdowns and saunas to onsite dining and reading rooms with complimentary Wi-Fi.

Keri had selected a smaller place known for leaving its patrons alone when they weren't getting services. She'd gone to the locker room, where she'd left her phone and real ID in a locker along with a fresh change of clothes. That way, while Keri was in Cave's office, the GPS on her phone said she was relaxing in a Koreatown spa.

Then she snuck out through a side door, leaving it unlocked using her patented tissue trick, got in her car, and headed downtown to violate multiple laws. When she returned, she used the same side door and returned to the locker room to undress for her 2:30 a.m. massage and body scrub.

At some point after the scrub and during the massage she fell asleep. When the masseuse woke her, it was 3:30 in the morning. She thanked the woman for the treatment she couldn't recall getting and retreated to the quiet room, where she crashed for three hours.

When her alarm buzzed her awake at 6:30 a.m., Keri didn't exactly feel refreshed. Her skin was raw and it wasn't just her injuries that hurt. Almost every muscle in her body ached. She knew she was supposed to have showered right after the treatment but she'd just been too tired. Whatever the woman had done to her while she slept, Keri was paying the price for it now.

She dragged herself to one of the showers and stood under the water for fifteen minutes, letting the warmth soothe her battered body. When she felt something approaching normal again, she got out and returned to the locker room.

Still in her robe, she took out the Android phone again. She turned it on, hoping that some password had magically auto-populated on the screen overnight. No such luck. The word "password" with the empty rectangle below it stared back at her, almost taunting her.

Trying to keep her cool, Keri returned it to her bag, changed into her fresh clothes—her standard slacks, shirt, and comfortable shoes—and headed out.

84

She arrived at Catherine Maroney Wexler's house ten minutes early and used the extra time to scarf down the blueberry muffin she'd grabbed at a coffee shop on the way over. As she sipped her coffee, she looked at the phone with the downloaded data one more time.

She knew this was getting ridiculous. It was starting to look like all the crazy risks she'd taken the night before were for nothing. She wasn't going to just have some "eureka!" moment and suddenly understand the inner workings of Jackson Cave's brain. And if she didn't know how he thought, there was no way she would ever break the code.

That's not quite true. I do know one person who might have some insight into how Cave's mind works.

Keri glanced at her watch. It was 7:58 a.m. There was no time to do anything before the interview with Kendra's sister. But after it was over, she knew exactly where she was going—to see a ghost.

CHAPTER SEVENTEEN

Keri tried to keep her cool despite her growing frustration. Catherine was surprisingly unhelpful for someone whose sister was missing. After welcoming Keri into what she announced as the drawing room of the old-fashioned, ornate Gothic Revival–style home, Catherine asked the housekeeper to bring them tea.

It struck Keri that this was a woman far more interested in appearances than her older sister. She had the same long, dark hair but she was more heavily made up, even at eight in the morning, than Kendra was in any picture Keri had seen.

She was slightly shorter and thinner, in a self-starved kind of way. She also looked like she'd had some plastic surgery, even though Keri guessed that Catherine was about the same age as her.

"So you moved out here after Kendra did?" Keri asked while they waited for the tea.

"Yes, she's three years older than me and I was inspired to pursue acting by her. Of course, by the time I got out here, she had given that up and was working as a junior publicist. I think her attempt at stardom left her with a bad taste in her mouth."

"You mean the photos?" Keri asked.

"How do you know about those?" Catherine asked, her eyes wide with surprise.

"It's my job to know these things. That's something I wanted to ask you about. My understanding is that you met Rafe Courtenay to make the most recent payment on Sunday. He said that was the first time anyone other than Kendra had dropped it off. Why the change?"

Catherine started to respond but stopped herself when the housekeeper brought in the tea. Only when the woman left did she answer.

"I have no idea. We'd only ever talked about those photos once, way back when I first moved out here and she was warning me about how unscrupulous people could be. I didn't even know she was being blackmailed. So it was a total surprise when she asked me to do this. All she said was that she had to deal with something important and it couldn't wait. I was really sketched out by the whole thing. But she sounded desperate so I agreed."

Catherine took a forceful sip of her tea, almost as if she were using its warmth to steady herself. Keri plunged ahead, not wanting to give her time to get too comfortable.

"She didn't give any details on what she was dealing with?"

"No," Catherine replied. "She said something about making things right. But other than that, she was pretty tight-lipped."

"Mrs. Wexler, we have indications that your sister may have just run away. Do you think that's possible? Could she could have just up and left town without telling anyone?"

Catherine put down her cup of tea and looked Keri squarely in the eyes.

"Listen, Detective, my sister and I aren't very close anymore. She thinks I sold my soul."

"Did you?' Keri asked, not mincing words.

Catherine paused for a moment before answering. She seemed to be genuinely pondering the question.

"I don't know. Acting was hard. And then I got married to a real estate developer who happens to be fabulously wealthy. I have two kids. I spend time at our club. I've had the occasional nip and tuck. She thought I gave up too easily on my dreams. But I'm pretty happy with my life."

"And what do you think of her?"

"I think my sister is an amazing woman. I mean, we're talking about a person who learned Spanish as a kid back in Phoenix so she could better connect with the illegal immigrant children at the shelter where she volunteered. But she's not the type to be satisfied with what she has. She was an amazing publicist but she got bored just smoothing things over for celebrities. So she started that foundation. She does amazing work to help those kids but she also wanted to travel the world, to try to coordinate satellite clinics in third world countries. But Jeremy was satisfied keeping the charity local. I think she got frustrated with that. Especially because of the kid issue."

Keri tried to keep her expression even as her breath quickened. In her experience, "kid issues" often played a prominent role in marital conflict.

"What kid issue?" she asked as nonchalantly as she could, not wanting to tip Catherine off to her heightened level of interest.

"She couldn't have them—they found out about five years ago. I think she threw herself into this work as a way to compensate. I know she got down sometimes. That's part of why she kept so busy. She hated being bored and Jeremy was more than satisfied just living the life they had. I think he was happy with it just being the two of them."

"Do you think that boredom could have manifested itself in other ways?" Keri asked.

"Are you asking if she might have had an affair?" Catherine asked point-blank.

"Yes," Keri said just as bluntly.

"Like I said, we weren't that close anymore so I wouldn't be the person to ask that question. Mags Merrywether would know more about Kendra's secrets. But it would surprise me. My sister had a strongly attuned moral compass. It's part of why we drifted apart. She thought mine didn't work as well."

"Okay. I think I have what I need. But there is one more thing."

"Yes?"

"You never really answered my question. Do you think Kendra might have just left?"

"No, Detective. The Kendra I knew never would have abandoned her life here, not unless she had a really good reason."

"Then if she didn't leave on her own, can you think of anyone who might have wanted to hurt her?"

Catherine sat quietly for a minute, deep in thought. When she looked up, Keri knew her answer before she spoke.

"I really can't," she finally said. "Most people—Jeremy, Mags, the kids she helped—adore her. We aren't best friends but I love her dearly. She's my big sister, you know? But someone with active animosity toward her? No, I can't think of anyone."

Keri thanked her and left quickly. As she walked back to her car, one frustrating thought stuck in her head.

Back to square one.

CHAPTER EIGHTEEN

Keri sat still, trying to hide her anxiousness as she waited for her guest to be brought into the cold, windowless, concrete-walled room.

The only amenities were the metal table in the center of the room and two metal benches on either side of it. All were bolted to the ground. Most everything was bolted down in the Twin Towers Correctional Facility in downtown Los Angeles.

That was the formal name of the county jail. It was supposed to be a way station for people awaiting trial or transfer to a long-term prison. But because of overcrowding, it often housed convicted criminals for weeks, months, and even years at a time, until a spot opened up somewhere else.

That was the situation of the man she was waiting for, Thomas "Ghost" Anderson. Anderson was a professional kidnapper who often abducted children for a fee. Sometimes his clients were couples uninterested in the formal adoption process. Other times, those hiring him had more nefarious intentions.

Keri had learned of him while searching for information on Evie's abductor. At one time, she even thought he might be the culprit, before meeting him in person. Despite eliminating him as a suspect, the more Keri had thought about it, the more likely it seemed that Evie's abductor had also been a pro. So she had decided that in order to catch a professional child abductor, it might help to pick the brain of another one.

And Anderson had indeed been helpful. He'd given her background on how the underground world of child abductions operated. He'd given her the street name—"the Collector"—of the man whose MO most closely matched how Evie was taken.

And most relevant to Keri now, he'd told her about how a few corrupt defense lawyers sometimes acted as intermediaries between abductors and potential clients. He mentioned one name in particular, his own attorney, Jackson Cave.

Why he'd been so forthcoming, Keri had no idea. She had promised to write a letter to the parole board on his behalf, something she hadn't done yet due to her showdown with Pachanga and subsequent hospitalization and recovery.

But that hardly seemed like enough of a reason for Anderson to give up so many trade secrets. She got the sense that he was playing some longer game. But for the time being, if he could help her, she didn't care what it was.

And she was pretty sure he could help her now. After all, as one of Jackson Cave's clients, he had spent many hours with the man. And Anderson was perceptive, scarily so. If anyone could hazard an educated guess as to what Cave's password might be, it was him.

The door to the room opened and Keri sat up straight, pushing any extraneous thoughts out of her head. When it came to Thomas Anderson, she needed to be at the top of her game.

He shuffled in, wearing shackles on his feet and handcuffs on his wrists. It was hard to be sure, but she thought she detected the slightest of limps.

Just like the last time they'd met, he wore his bright orange prisoner jumpsuit. Just like last time, his thick black hair was parted neatly, as if he'd wet it down in anticipation of their meeting.

But unlike last time when he'd already been sitting down in the room waiting for her, she could now gauge his height and build. He wasn't especially tall, maybe five foot eight. But he was squarely built. And for a man in his fifties, he'd clearly made an effort to stay in shape. Even under the loose jumpsuit, she could tell he regularly used the jail's weight room.

If possible, it looked like he had gotten even more tattoos in the two weeks since she'd last seen him. Almost every visible inch of skin on the right side of his body, from his fingers to his ear, was covered with them. And now there was a small bandage on the outside of his wrist that she suspected covered a new piece of art. Interestingly, the left side of his body was completely devoid of ink.

Keri looked at his face and saw his dark eyes studying her closely. She could see him doing some kind of mental calculation. She didn't take offense, as that's exactly what she'd been doing to him.

"New tattoo?" she asked, nodding in the direction of his wrist as the guard attached his shackles to a bar on the table.

"A sparrow," he said. "I'd show you but it's still too raw and bloody to really appreciate it. How are the ribs?"

"Still sore," she answered, trying to hide her surprise. The nature of her injuries hadn't made it into news reports and she hadn't moved at all since he entered the room. "How did you know...?"

"Your breathing is more shallow than the last time you visited me, which indicates either a rib injury or a muscle pull in that area. And the way you're carefully keeping your arm away from your side, so you don't accidentally bump them, suggests ribs."

"Very perceptive, especially for a man who should probably be using a walker. Is it just arthritis or did someone sweep the leg in the yard?"

Anderson smiled, revealing a mouth of full of gleaming white teeth.

"Touché, Detective Locke. In fact, my leg injury was the result of an altercation. I got it defending your honor."

"What?"

"There was a report on the news about your run-in with Alan Pachanga. Congratulations, by the way. Another prisoner saw you at the press conference, sitting there in your wheelchair, pleading for help finding your daughter, and said you seemed like a real bitch."

"I am a real bitch," Keri admitted.

"Be that as it may, I thought it was quite inappropriate of him to say it and I told him so. He took umbrage with my comment. A squabble ensued, which is how I suffered the sprained knee you noticed."

"Did you get in a few licks at least?" Keri asked, suspecting that Thomas Anderson, even at his age, could do some serious damage.

"I should say so. He's still in the infirmary. Something about broken fingers, a shattered kneecap, and a hairline fracture of the skull."

He listed off the injuries as though they were items on a grocery shopping list. It reminded Keri that despite his genteel manner the man across from her was very dangerous.

"Wow," she said, trying to act unperturbed, "I'm surprised they let you have visitors after that."

"They wouldn't normally. I've actually been in solitary confinement since it happened and will be for the next two weeks. But I guess they make exceptions for visits from law enforcement. So I suppose I should thank you for allowing me to get some comparatively fresh air and stretch my legs a bit."

He tried to lean back in his chair, as if attempting to luxuriate in his surroundings, but the shackles prevented him from getting too comfortable.

"Well, it just so happens I know a way you can thank me," Keri told him.

"Just saying 'thank you' isn't enough?" he asked, with just a hint of feigned insult.

Keri wanted him to know she was serious so she leaned in and spoke plainly.

"I'm looking for something a little more substantial."

Anderson smiled ever so slightly, enjoying a lingering pause before finally responding.

"It would be my pleasure. Can I assume that you'll reciprocate in some way? After all, the parole board can only process so many letters of recommendation."

Keri couldn't tell if he was genuinely unaware that she had yet to write the letter or was testing her.

Best to come clean with this guy. If he stops trusting me, he'll never help.

"About that," she said, "I've been a bit busy since we last met, what with finding Ashley Penn's abductor, getting in a life-or-death fight with him, and spending a week in the hospital. So I haven't had a chance to get to your letter just yet. I didn't want to rush it, you know."

Anderson nodded, seemingly untroubled by the delay.

"I appreciate your honesty, Detective Locke. But it would be nice if you could get to it soon. Maybe by the time I'm released from solitary. I have a parole hearing in November and I'd love to add it to the official record."

"You really think it's going to make any difference when you'll have just been in the hole for a month?"

"You'd be surprised," he replied. "I can be very persuasive when I want to be."

She already knew that to be the case. When she'd first reviewed his records, she saw that he had acted as his own counsel at his most recent trial. Apparently, he'd been so convincing that if the case against him hadn't been ironclad, he might have gotten a hung jury.

"If you don't mind me saying, Mr. Anderson, I'm less surprised that you can be convincing than I am that you're in here in the first place. You seem so meticulous. I'm amazed you got caught."

Anderson chuckled softly before answering.

"I think meticulous is a wonderful word to describe me, Detective Locke. Perhaps that's why I became a librarian."

"You were a librarian?" Keri couldn't keep the shock out of her voice.

"For over thirty years, the last ten at the Los Angeles Central Library. Have you ever been? It's a real jewel. As to my getting caught and convicted while being so very meticulous, that is quite a stunner. Almost suspicious, don't you think?"

Keri tried to let it all sink in. Anderson having been a librarian was unexpected enough. But he seemed to be suggesting that his incarceration might be partly of his own design. It was all too much to process at once. And none of it was relevant to the reason she had come here. She needed to get this conversation back on track.

"I will definitely write that letter soon," she promised, forcing herself to maintain a polite, playful tone, despite her growing impatience. "But as I mentioned, I could use your help with something, if you're so inclined."

"Of course. I'll do what I can, within reason. What is it?"

Keri glanced up at the guard standing in the corner of the room.

"I need a moment," she told him. The man didn't look enthused to leave but he did so without a word.

"Oh, this feels very cloak and dagger," Anderson said almost gleefully.

"It's kind of sensitive."

Anderson leaned in, getting as close to her as the shackles would allow. His next words were spoken in a whisper.

"Then you should know that even with the guard out of the room, the walls have ears."

"I guess I'll have to be cryptic then," Keri replied, refusing to whisper herself but definitely lowering her voice. "Do you recall that the last time I was here, we discussed your... friend?"

"I do."

His voice was pleasant but the playfulness had disappeared from his eyes. Keri proceeded carefully, not wanting to spook him.

"I got the impression that you have a strong sense of him; that in your time together, you might have developed some insight into how his thought process works."

"I may have," he said, revealing nothing.

Keri debated whether to continue. Something about laying her cards on the table with a man like The Ghost made her deeply uncomfortable. But she didn't really have much choice. She was out of options.

"So if this friend wanted to protect some digital information, to keep it well hidden from prying eyes by requiring that the information be retrieved through a written key of some kind, do you have any ideas as to what that key might be?"

"You've come to the right person, Detective Locke. It so happens that I'm quite confident that I know what his...key is."

"That's great," Keri said, unable to keep the excitement out of her voice. "What is it?"

"I can't tell you."

CHAPTER NINETEEN

"What?" Keri demanded, her voice a mix of anger and confusion.

"I'm afraid I can't reveal that information," he repeated.

"What do you mean, you can't reveal it? Why not?"

"The information I shared with you at our last visit was, if not common knowledge, at least easily accessible. Even if I was formally acting as a 'rat,' it was forgivable because what I told you wasn't proprietary."

"So you're saying you'd feel guilty if you told me what I need to know now because it's more secret?" Keri asked, dumbfounded.

"Not at all. Guilt isn't an emotion I waste time with. How could I do the things I did if guilt was a factor? I'm saying that if I gave you what you're looking for, it could be traced back to me. And my friend has many resources in this facility, among both prisoners and guards. I suspect that if word got out that I had assisted you, I wouldn't make it to my parole hearing."

"So you're just covering your ass?"

"Can you blame me, Detective Locke? Even at my advanced age, I think it's a lovely derriere. And I'd like to keep it in one piece."

Keri shook her head, not amused. She'd come so close. She had the data to find Evie in her possession. She was sitting across from a man who could give her the password that would let her access it. And he wasn't talking.

She looked back at him, trying to decide if it was worth going at him again in some other way. But she could tell it was a waste of time. His face had gone stony and the glint of playfulness had left his eyes.

"Guard!" she called out. As she waited for him to return, Anderson suddenly leaned forward with unfamiliar intensity in his eyes.

"Keri," he whispered slowly, using her first name for the only time she could recall. "Listen very closely. I want to help you but I can't. You must understand how these things work. Jackson Cave is the key to this place. You've got it all backward. It would be capital for you to find what you're looking for. In truth, you already have everything you need. Mark my words."

The guard stepped inside and Anderson stood up without having to be asked. He looked at Keri with a level of deliberation she'd never seen before. As the guard directed him out of the room, he turned back and repeated himself.

"Mark my words." And then he was gone

*

Keri turned over Anderson's last strange comments in her head as she drove back to the station. It was as if he'd turned into a different person in those last few moments. She couldn't understand what had happened to him.

Her thoughts were interrupted by a call from Edgerton.

"You close to being back?" he asked when she picked up.

"I should be there in twenty minutes. Why?"

"Hillman has called an all-hands meeting. It starts in fifteen. I'll try to stall him."

"Why didn't he call me himself?" she demanded.

"I'm pretty sure he did."

Keri looked at her phone and saw two missed messages. They must have come in when she was with Anderson. The guards made her turn in her phone and gun when she entered. She'd been so wrapped up in trying to understand what was up with Anderson that she'd forgotten to check them.

"Is he pissed?" she asked, already knowing the answer.

"Is he ever *not* pissed?" Edgerton replied.

Twenty minutes later, Keri walked into Conference Room A. Everyone else was already assembled. Edgerton was in the corner, showing Hillman some piece of paper, gesticulating meaningfully.

But as soon as he saw Keri, he stopped and went to his seat, giving her a little smile. She realized that whatever he'd been showing Hillman must have been intended just to distract him until she got there. She smiled back gratefully.

"Now that everyone's here," Hillman said accusingly as he stared at Keri, "let's begin. Detective Brody, can you catch us up on where the investigation stands now?"

Brody, who had been chomping on an everything bagel, stood up and, oblivious to the bits of poppy seeds and bagel crumbs stuck to his tie, walked to the front of the room.

"So last night, we went to the Burlingames' big fundraiser and interviewed a bunch of rich dicks. Everybody had the same story— 'They're a great couple.' Nobody could think why she might just up and bail. No sign of it. No real marital problems.

"I had to talk to the doctor for a while. He held it together okay up on stage giving his speech. But afterward, he cornered me and started asking all these questions about what he could do to help. He was a frickin' wreck. I felt for the guy but what everyone said about him is true. He's boring. And according to the guests there, she's not. Supposedly they seem to like it that way. But I guess she was more bored than people thought because everything's pointing to her adios-ing town, right, baby boy?"

Edgerton, looking annoyed at the moniker, started to open his mouth, but Hillman shut him down.

"We'll get to that in a minute. And Brody, try to be professional, okay?" He turned his attention to Keri. "Locke, you've been AWOL all morning. What have you been doing with your time?"

"I spent the morning interviewing Kendra's younger sister, Catherine," Keri said, refusing to take the bait. "She also indicated that the marriage seemed to be fine, although she admitted that she and Kendra hadn't been very close in recent years. She also found it hard to believe that her sister would just bail on her life. She was too committed to what she was doing."

"Or not," Hillman said, turning to Kevin. "Catch us up, Edgerton."

"Yes sir. We recently learned that Kendra Burlingame's bank account has been closed and all the money transferred to an account in Switzerland."

"How much was in there?" asked Detective Jerry Cantwell, an old-timer who was almost as fossilized as Brody.

"A little over seventy grand. But what's weird is that it could have been a lot more. Both Burlingames have their own separate checking accounts, as well as a joint one. She could have pulled as much as she liked out of the joint account too but the money she took came exclusively from her account."

"How much was in the joint account?" Keri asked.

"Three hundred thirty-two thousand."

"Holy shit!" Brody shouted. "She just left all that money on the table?"

"Maybe she didn't want to screw over her husband," Suarez volunteered. "If this was just her feeling like she needed to start over, it makes sense that she wouldn't want to leave him destitute. It doesn't seem like she wanted to ruin his life, just reboot hers."

"Was anything else taken from other accounts?" Hillman asked.

"No," Edgerton answered. "All of her investments are untouched. But accessing them would have taken longer and been more complicated. Maybe she didn't want to risk tipping someone off to what she was doing."

"Good work. What about the whole Palm Springs bus station thing?"

"Oh, I asked Patterson to take that over so I could focus on the financials."

"Okay, where are we at, Patterson?" Hillman asked.

Detective Garrett Patterson, a quiet, smallish guy in his mid-thirties, cleared his throat. His nickname was Grunt Work, mainly because he didn't mind doing it. He seemed to get off on checking endless hours of surveillance footage, reviewing database records, or cold-calling potential witnesses.

"I've gone through the footage from the Phoenix bus station and there's no record of the woman in the video at the Palm Springs station getting off there. I also checked every other stop that had security footage—Tucson, El Paso, San Antonio, Houston, New Orleans—"

"We get it, Patterson," Brody interrupted. "Cut to the chase."

"She's not visible exiting the bus at any location along the way or when they stopped for good in Orlando."

"So what does that mean?" Brody asked, visibly frustrated. "Are you saying she's still hiding out on that bus?"

"No. There were lots of other stops at small stations without cameras. She could have gotten off at any of them and we'd never know."

"What about the bus itself?" Keri asked. "Doesn't it have cameras?"

"It has one near the driver's rearview mirror. But it wasn't working."

"Disabled?" asked Edgerton.

"Unknown. But it was working fine for all that bus's trips last week. There's more."

"Good news, I'm sure," Detective Sterling, Cantwell's partner, muttered sarcastically.

"Afraid not. Palm Springs PD collected every snow globe from that gift shop at the bus station to test for prints."

"Why not just the one with the Palm Springs façade?" asked Keri.

"There were four Palm Springs snow globes and they couldn't be sure which one Kendra grabbed. They're testing those first but they took them all just to be safe."

"What did they find?" Suarez asked.

"A *lot* of prints. You can imagine how many people walked through that store and picked up those globes. Apparently they don't get cleaned that often. Their forensic guys are working through them to identify everyone they can but it's a slow process."

"Thanks, Patterson," Hillman said, stepping forward. "So you can see, we're at a bit of an impasse here. We're not dropping the case just yet. I want to pull the strings on these outstanding issues—the prints, more interviews with the doctor's co-workers, following up on that Swiss bank account to see if anyone comes collecting, assuming the bank will cooperate. We'll look into all of that and have another all-hands tomorrow morning, bright and early at eight a.m. But if nothing firm has turned up by then…"

"Sir," Keri started to say but stopped when she saw the look in Hillman's eyes. He continued.

"If we don't have anything by then, we may have to close this case, whether you want to or not, whether her husband wants us to or not. He has the resources to hire his own investigator if he chooses. But as you all know, if Kendra Burlingame decided to check out of her life and hasn't done anything nefarious along the way, there's not much we can do. We're in the business of investigating crimes and there doesn't seem to be a crime committed here. That is all."

The meeting broke up and everyone else hurried out, not wanting to incur Hillman's wrath. Keri stayed in her seat.

"Anything you care to add, Locke?" he asked curtly as he gathered up his papers.

"No sir," she said, getting up and heading back to her desk.

Hillman was right. All the evidence indicated that Kendra had skipped town to either get away from her current life or just start a new one. Just because everyone Keri had spoken to said it wasn't like her didn't mean it wasn't possible. Keri's job often consisted of arresting people no one thought capable of the crime they'd committed.

She sat down at her desk and allowed herself to take a mental break from the case. She still had that itch in the back of her brain, saying something wasn't quite right about it. But there wasn't much she could do until forensics came back and there was no point in doing what she so often did: obsessing.

Keri pulled out the old Android phone with Cave's data and stared at it again.

So this is my life? If I'm not obsessing over one case, I have to obsess over another?

Apparently it was, she had to admit to herself as she stared blankly at the phone, the word "password" emblazoned tauntingly on the screen.

All she needed was one word to open up a whole world of information on the underground child abduction trade. If she could get just one word, it would unlock everything else. It was the key.

Then something popped into her head, something Thomas Anderson had said when he was rambling at the end of their meeting: Jackson Cave was the key.

What if he meant that literally? I did ask what the key was.

She cast her mind back to their conversation. It was less than an hour ago and she could still recall it almost completely:

You must understand how these things work. Jackson Cave is the key to this place. You've got it all backward. It would be capital for you to find what you're looking for. In truth, you already have everything you need. Mark my words.

Jackson Cave is the key. What if that wasn't just hyperbole but the literal truth? Anderson had said to mark his words. He'd said it twice. It was the last thing he'd told her, almost pleading with her to get it. What if Cave's *name* was the key, the password?

But the password could only be one word, not two. Keri shook the doubt out of her head and forced herself to focus on Anderson's words.

You've got it all backward.

As quickly as she could, Keri typed in Cave's name backward as one word: evacnoskcaj.

The screen blinked before displaying the message "invalid password" in red letters.

That's not the whole clue. He also said "It would be capital for you to find what you're looking for."

"It would be capital" sounded ridiculous, like he had suddenly joined the cast of some Gilbert and Sullivan musical. But he would have known that. He wanted it to sound weird, to draw attention to it—capital.

Keri tried the backward name again, this time in all capital letters: EVACNOSKCAJ.

The screen blinked again. After a long second, a new phrase popped up:

"Password accepted."

CHAPTER TWENTY

Keri stared at the screen for several seconds, refusing to blink for fear that what she saw might disappear. She couldn't believe her eyes.

On the screen was a long list, organized in a way she couldn't immediately understand, with numeric codes scattered throughout. But among the codes were what clearly seemed to be initials and dates.

After a few minutes it became clear that the organizing principle of the list was the abductors. There would be a heading with what looked to be initials. Below that were dated entries with the coded numbers she couldn't understand. She suspected that they referred to the specifics of the abduction or perhaps the identity of the client or even the child.

Keri scrolled down hungrily, looking for anything that looked familiar. Then she froze. On the screen in front of her was a date—9/18/11. That was the date Evie was taken.

The date was followed by a series of numbers and letters that meant nothing to her. She scrolled back up to see what the heading title was and gave out an audible gasp at what she saw.

Suarez, one desk over, looked up in alarm. She gave him a half-smile.

"Big sale at Target," she said. He nodded, uninterested, and returned to his paperwork.

Keri's eyes returned to the screen, disbelieving. The header was titled simply "Ctr." It could stand for anything but one reasonable possibility was that it stood for "Collector." Even more promising than that, following those letters was an e-mail address.

After all these years, was it possible that she was just an e-mail away from contacting the man who'd kidnapped her child? Was it really possible?

I guess I'm about to find out.

Keri quickly set up a dummy Gmail account and prepared to type a message. But as her fingers rested on the keyboard, she could feel the anxiety creeping into her gut. What if she screwed this up and the guy never responded? What if he shut down the account?

Borderline angry with herself, she shook the thoughts from her head.

Keep the emotion out of it. Forget about Evie. Just set something up with the suspect. Do your job.

She wanted to keep it simple and non-threatening. She didn't even know if the address was legitimate. But if it was, she wanted to keep her message vague while still piquing the Collector's interest. Finally she typed a brief message:

"Need some work done. You come recommended. JC speaks highly. Would like to discuss."

Keri looked at the e-mail repeatedly, trying to find some flaw that would give her away. But it seemed pretty good. Her email name, Guy347BD5, was randomly chosen and hopefully gave the impression that as a potential client, she was careful.

You're stalling now. Just hit Send.

She did so, then wrote a separate e-mail to Edgerton asking him to try to trace the e-mail for "Ctr." She doubted he'd find anything. This guy was a professional and she suspected he was pretty good at covering his tracks or he'd have been caught long ago. Still, it was worth a shot.

And since she was slightly paranoid that "Ctr." might somehow be able to tell his e-mail address was being traced, she warned Edgerton that the trace was highly sensitive and not to do anything that might reveal to the subject they were investigating it.

With that done, and after twenty minutes of constantly refreshing her mail, Keri decided her obsession wasn't constructive and she needed to take a mental break.

Maybe a visit with Ray can de-jangle my nerves.

The idea gave her a warm feeling. She grabbed her stuff and hurried to her car, doing her best to ignore her protesting ribs.

On the drive over, Keri tried to clear her head but it was no good. Her thoughts kept returning to the list and to the man who'd designed it, Jackson Cave.

Part of her wanted to drive to his office right now, arrest him, and sort the rest out later. But after a few deep breaths to clear her head, she remembered why that would be a terrible idea.

First, the list wasn't actually proof of anything, at least not yet. It was just a series of numbers and letters. To her, it was clear that they represented initials, dates, and contact information. But that might not be clear to everyone, certainly not to a prosecutor.

Beyond that, using the list to try to bust Cave would implicate her as well. She had gotten it by breaking into the private office of an officer of the court. Even if a case could be made against Jackson Cave, she was guaranteeing her own arrest and likely conviction.

But even that would have been worth it if she thought it would help get Evie back. Unfortunately, she doubted it would. The second that Cave's arrest made the news, the Collector would go to ground and she'd lose the best lead she'd found since her daughter was taken.

Cave was simply a means to an end. And that end was finding the Collector in the hope that he would lead her to Evie. Anything that interfered with that goal was a non-starter. So she'd have to leave Cave be for now.

Keri walked into Ray's hospital room an hour later to find him napping. She hadn't spoken to him since calling him late last night on the way to Cave's office. For all he knew, she might have been in jail for breaking and entering.

She sat quietly in the uncomfortable hard-backed chair in the corner of the room, watching her friend nap, periodically checking her phone for an e-mail reply from the Collector. Something about his slow, rhythmic breathing relaxed her and she felt the anxiety of the day slip away. Even the soreness from her injuries and the ill-advised overnight massage faded.

Is this how I would feel if I lay next to him at night, lulled to sleep by the soothing sound of him?

She stayed like that for a while, just sitting and wondering. Suddenly she heard a clang and startled, realizing she'd drifted off to sleep. A nurse had plopped a tray on the adjustable table connected to the bed and the sound made Ray stir. Keri looked the clock on the wall. It was 12:30 p.m. exactly. She'd been asleep for over a half hour. She checked her e-mail again—nothing.

"Time for lunch, Detective Sands," the nurse said in an overly chipper voice that made Keri want to slug her. "Do you need some help sitting up?"

"No thanks. I've got it, Janet," he said groggily. He pulled himself upright and saw Keri in the corner for the first time. He smiled at her but didn't speak until Janet left.

"I'm glad to see you here rather than being asked to help pony up for your bail money," he said once the door closed, leaving them alone.

"You joke but that was closer to being a reality than I care to think about."

"So I take it you didn't turn around and go home like you promised?"

"Actually I had a hankering for a late-night massage and body scrub so I spent the night in Koreatown."

"I don't even know where to start with that one," he said. "Is that a euphemism? Should I ask if you got a happy ending?"

"I really did get a massage," Keri assured him. "But I also managed to run another errand and you could say that, despite a few uncertain moments, I did get a very happy ending."

"This conversation is making me a little uncomfortable," Ray said. "Could you be cryptic in a less creepy way?"

"You started it. But okay. Yes, I made a pit stop and managed to find an item I needed. In fact, I just figured out how to use it."

Ray's eyes widened.

"You broke the code?" he mouthed silently.

Keri nodded before adding in a hushed voice.

"I think so."

"So what happens now?" he whispered.

"Well, it turns out that there are e-mails on this thing. And one of them looks like it belongs to the guy I've been looking for. So I reached out."

"You did what?" Ray demanded, no longer whispering.

"Keep your voice down, Ray. I created an anonymous e-mail account and contacted the guy. I said I needed help with a job."

"Have you heard back?"

The question caused her to look again. Still no reply.

"Not yet. But I sent it not even two hours ago."

"So what happens if he gets back to you?" he asked.

"I guess I'll cross that bridge when I come to it."

"You can't go after this guy alone, you know. There's no telling what he's capable of."

"I know that, Raymond," she said, trying to scold him into submission.

"Don't act like I'm insulting you. Going after suspects alone is practically a job description for you. Seriously, you won't make a move without talking to me first, right?"

"Of course not," she lied.

They sat quietly for a few minutes as Ray picked at his lunch of chicken and rice soup, fruit cocktail, and the saddest side salad Keri had ever seen. After a while, Ray gave up and pushed the tray away.

"How's the Burlingame case going?" he asked.

"Stalled. All signs point to her having run off. It doesn't feel right to me but I don't have anything firm to base that on. We're waiting for some fingerprints and surveillance camera footage to come back. But it's not promising."

"So what are you doing with the downtime? Is the houseboat all packed up?" he asked.

Keri raised her eyebrows quizzically.

"You're kidding, right? I've been working a case. I'm making late night stops to…visit folks. I just took off my shoulder sling yesterday and every time I take a deep breath, it feels like someone's jabbing a knife in my rib cage."

"You're looking for sympathy from me on the walking wounded front?" he asked, disbelieving.

"I'm just saying I haven't had a lot time to bubble wrap my valuables. Besides, I don't have a new place yet. So you know, cart before the horse."

"I've been looking for places for you. I think I may have found something."

"Really? Where?"

"Playa del Rey. Not too far from the station. It's in the same general area as the houseboat so you could still go to your favorite grocery store. It's pretty small. And old. And kind of ugly if the photos I saw are accurate. But it's a two-bedroom."

"How much is it?" Keri asked warily.

"The rent is reasonable. It's above a little dive restaurant on Culver, about six blocks from the beach. I know the owner and he's willing to give you a deal. You should go check it out today, especially since you have a bit of extra time."

He handed her a sheet of paper with the address.

"That's not a bad idea. Maybe I'll head over there now."

"I think you should. I'll let Rene know you're coming."

Keri stood up, walked over to Ray's bedside, and put her hand on his arm.

"Thank you," she said. "You still supposed to get out of here at the end of the week?"

"That's the hope."

"Maybe I can drive you home. We could get some coffee and talk about stuff."

"Stuff?" he asked.

"Yeah, stuff."

"I would love to talk about stuff," he said. "Stuff is one of my favorite topics."

"Okay," Keri said, taking her hand off his arm and heading for the door. "That's about enough of that. I'm going to go check this place out. You take it easy, okay?"

"I will," he promised, and, shouting after her as she left the room, added, "I'm just going to be here, thinking about stuff."

She couldn't fight the grin that forced itself onto her face as she walked down the hall. When she reached the elevator, she checked her phone. The smile immediately disappeared.

The Collector had replied to her e-mail.

CHAPTER TWENTY ONE

Keri tore out of the hospital parking structure without regard for signs, other cars, or even people. Her heart was pumping fast and her hands gripped the steering wheel tight, turning her fingers white.

The Collector, or whoever was behind the e-mail she'd received, had given her only a brief window to get to the location he'd selected. The message had been short and to the point:

1:30 today. 3rd street promenade. santa monica. Just south of arizona and third. metal chair on east side of street next to sculpture. wear red shirt. sit down. wait.

She immediately replied, "Okay."

The e-mail didn't give her much time, which was obviously by design. If she'd been downtown or in the San Fernando Valley when she received it, there was no way she could have made it. As it was, the hospital in Beverly Hills wasn't that far. Still, Keri only had about forty-five minutes to drive to Santa Monica, park, and find someone to sit in the metal chair at the appointed time.

It couldn't be her, of course. If the Collector saw her, he might recognize her from all those years ago, on that day when he had taken Evie from her. If he got even a hint that the mother of a girl he'd abducted was in the area, he'd be gone and the e-mail address would be blown as a resource. And she couldn't postpone the meet. Any attempt to change the terms would risk alienating the Collector and that wasn't a risk she was willing to take.

So she was stuck. She had to find a believable decoy—someone the Collector would see sitting on that metal chair and believe could be a potential client in the market for an abduction.

And she'd have to wing it, selecting her potential decoy based on little more than that he looked the part. This wasn't how she wanted this operation to proceed. But she wasn't in charge and she'd just have to adapt as best she could.

As she barreled down Wilshire Boulevard, Keri decided to use the time to try to even up the odds. She called Edgerton to see if he'd made any progress tracing the e-mail address.

"I'm sorry, Keri," he said. "I keep hitting dead ends. And I'm worried that if I try to force my way in, your subject may get an alert. This guy's sneaky and I'm worried I may set off an electronic tripwire if I go any further. Who is he anyway?"

"I can't really get into it right now," Keri answered, as much to protect Edgerton as to guard her own secrets. "Go ahead and drop it for the time being and we'll regroup later. Just focus on the Burlingame stuff for now, okay?"

"No problem," he said.

Keri was about to hang up when she had an idea.

"Hey, Kevin, is Officer Castillo around?" she asked.

"I think she's off duty today but I can text you her private cell if you want."

"Do that," Keri said as she zipped under the 405 Freeway overpass. She was less than fifteen minutes from the Promenade but it was almost 1 p.m. At this rate, she wouldn't have much time to set things in motion once she got there.

Edgerton's text came in and Keri punched in Castillo's phone number.

"Jamie here," said a cheery voice.

"Officer Castillo, it's Detective Keri Locke. I'm sorry to bother you on your day off. But I may need to ask a favor."

"Of course, Detective. What can I do to help?" Castillo responded without a moment's hesitation.

"Hold on a second," Keri said.

She looked at the time again—1:02 p.m. Borderline desperate, she grabbed the siren from her passenger seat, turned it on, and put it on her roof. Then she rolled up her window

"Sorry about that," she continued. "You said you used to work in West LA Division. Does that mean you happen to live in the area?"

"You bet. My commute to the station was less than five minutes."

"Any chance you're in the vicinity right now?" Keri asked hopefully.

"I just got out of a movie in Westwood," Castillo answered happily.

Keri blasted through the intersection at Centinela Avenue, honking at an oblivious pedestrian in the crosswalk.

"Are you carrying your service revolver?" she asked.

There was a brief pause on the other end of the line.

"I am," Castillo answered, her voice now completely serious.

"Okay, Officer, I'm going to make an unusual request of you. If you decline, no hard feelings. But I could really use a hand and it's kind of time-sensitive."

Less than a second passed before she got her answer.

"What do you need?"

"Get to your car and drive to the Third Street Promenade. I'll explain en route."

"I'm starting my car now, Detective. Fill me in."

Keri hesitated for second, aware that opening up like this could put her at risk. But at this point she was out of options. She dove in.

"All right, here's the short version. You know my daughter was abducted five years ago. I have a lead on a potential suspect. I'm supposed to meet him on the Promenade near the corner of Third and Arizona. He thinks I'm a potential client who wants to pay to have someone abducted."

Keri was about to cross the intersection at 26th Street when a pickup truck, ignoring her siren, blasted through. She hit her brakes hard, coming within three feet of T-boning the idiot. Rivers of adrenaline shot through her arms and up to her fingertips. All her extremities were tingling.

"Are you okay, Detective Locke?" Castillo yelled over the phone.

"Mostly," Keri answered. "Where was I?"

"You're a potential client."

"Right. So I'm headed there now. Since the guy would recognize me, I have to find someone to serve as my emissary and give this abductor a message. I'm hoping he'll consider that a sign that his potential client is careful and can be trusted. Does all that make sense?"

"Absolutely," Castillo said. "So you want me to be the emissary?"

Keri had briefly considered that possibility before she called but had dismissed it as too risky.

"No, I think he'd be more comfortable if the decoy was a guy. I'm going to have to find someone credible when I get down there. I need you for backup. I want you to position yourself on an adjacent roof where you can see everything. If the guy shows up, you can feed me intel from your vantage point. If things go south somehow, I'm not alone trying to take him down."

She stopped talking and realized Castillo hadn't said anything in a while. She worried the younger woman was getting cold feet.

"You okay, Jamie?" she asked.

"Yeah. I'm just getting the sense that this isn't a department-sanctioned stakeout."

Keri fought the urge to convince the impressionable officer to throw caution to the wind.

"It's not," she admitted. "That's the other thing. This whole plan is a rogue operation. I came by the information about this guy through questionable methods. Lieutenant Hillman would definitely disapprove if he knew. My plan isn't exactly meticulously planned out. And it's potentially dangerous. So like I said, no hard feelings if you pass. In fact, I recommend it."

Keri passed Lincoln Boulevard. She was only minutes from the Promenade now. Biting her lip, she waited for Castillo's response. The silence seemed to last an eternity. Finally the rookie officer replied.

"Text me when you get down there and let me know exactly where you want me to set up."

"You sure?" Keri asked, giving her one last out. "I kind of called you because no one who's been on this job for a while would even consider doing it."

"I should be there in ten minutes," Castillo answered and hung up without another word.

Keri smiled to herself as she turned off the siren and returned it to the passenger seat. She made a quick left onto 5th Street and pulled into a covered parking garage. She looked at the time—1:10. There was still a lot of work to do and only twenty minutes to do it.

CHAPTER TWENTY TWO

Once she parked, Keri allowed herself thirty seconds to take a few breaths and refocus. She was wired and that could lead to mistakes. She couldn't afford mistakes.

Grabbing a sheet of paper from a notepad, she wrote a short message in basic block lettering. It read:

"Sent this stranger as a go-between. Forgive my caution. Troublesome co-worker needs a long vacation. Could use assistance. Please e-mail."

It wasn't a literary masterpiece, but under the circumstances, it would do. Keri put her hair up in a bun, threw on a cap and sunglasses and, now in a perfunctory disguise, stepped into a vintage boutique on 4th Street to buy a cheap red T-shirt. The least expensive one she could find was $30 but she didn't have time to keep looking so she got it.

After a pit stop at an ATM to grab $200, she rushed over to 3rd Street, one block south of Arizona, and looked around for a likely candidate for the job.

She found the guy she was looking for leaning against a magazine rack at a newsstand in the middle of the promenade, perusing a woodworking magazine. He looked to be in his mid-twenties. He had a wispy beard and wore a gray T-shirt that said "check out my wood."

But instead of approaching him directly, Keri decided to take an extra level of precaution. She'd use two decoys. That way, if the Collector asked the woodworking fan who sent him there, her identity would still be protected.

She searched the area for the other half of her team. It took a minute before she found someone acceptable. Finally she saw her stand-in—a chunky guy in his early forties with plastered down blond hair and a turtleneck sweater. He was sitting on a bench by a fountain, scrolling through his phone as he finished a sandwich.

She only had ten minutes until the designated time and had to move fast. Walking up to the sandwich guy, she put on her most charming smile. She stood over him for a second, waiting for him to notice her. When he did, he seemed startled, which was what Keri was going for.

"Hey there," she said as sweetly as she could.

"Hi?" he asked more than said.

"Are you busy right now?"

"I was just finishing my lunch. I have to be back at work at one thirty."

"Oh, where do you work?"

"At GameStop."

"Cool. Anyway, it sounds like you still have a few minutes. I was wondering if you could do me a teensy favor?"

"What is it?" he asked warily.

"It's going to sound weird. But it's harmless. And if you do it, I'll give you a hundred dollars."

"I don't know. This sounds sketchy." He looked like he was about to bolt.

"Listen. I'll tell you the favor. If you think it's too crazy, just say no. But if it just sounds standard weird and you say yes, you get a hundred bucks. Nothing to lose, right?"

"Tell me the favor and I'll see."

"I want you to go over to that guy," she said, pointing at the woodworker. "You need to get him to put on this red shirt and go sit down in a metal chair by the sculpture near the end of the block up there. You can't mention me or even look at me. The guy has to think it was your idea."

"Why would he do that?"

"Because you're going to give him one hundred dollars," Keri said in her best spokesmodel voice.

"Why don't you ask him to do it yourself and save a hundred bucks?"

"What's your name, sweetie?"

"Randall."

"Randy, I'm Carol, by the way. You may be a little too smart for your own good. I have my reasons. All you need to know is that if you successfully get him to do what I asked, you get five twenties. Are you up for it or not?"

"I guess so."

"What a trouper. Now there's one more little thing."

"I knew there was a catch," Randall said indignantly.

"It's not a catch. You just need to tell him that he has to sit in the chair at exactly one thirty and he needs to stay there until at least one forty-five. If anyone approaches him, he should give the person this note. He's not to read it. Now that's only seven minutes away, so you better get cracking."

Randall took the money and folded note and started to head over to the other guy when Keri thought of an added incentive.

"Hey, Randy, if you make this happen, I'll give you my number." She winked for emphasis, fighting down her gag reflex.

His beleaguered expression changed to a combination of excitement and fearfulness. But it seemed to do the trick. He nodded and walked toward Woody with what appeared to be more purpose.

She moved behind the fountain and watched as Randy GameStop chatted up Woody. As she suspected, Woody didn't need much convincing. The moment he saw the money he was all in. He put on the shirt, snagged the bills and note, and immediately headed in the direction of the chair.

"He went for it," Randy said when he returned.

"I kind of figured. Did you tell him to sit down at exactly one thirty p.m.?"

"Just like you said," Randy assured her. "So can I get my money now?"

"Of course," she said, handing him the bills.

"And your number—can I still get that?"

"You know what, Randy, why don't you give me yours? You seem like a really good guy. But a girl can't be too careful these days."

"But you promised," Randy whined.

"Don't you have to be at work in five minutes? I don't want you to get in trouble, Randy. Give me your number and I promise I'll get in touch, okay?"

Randy gave it to her, although his sour expression indicated he had no confidence that she'd call. When he headed off, Keri made her way as quickly as she could to the Coffee Bean & Tea Leaf across from the metal chair, where she could watch events unfold without being seen.

As she walked, she texted Castillo to find out if she'd found a good observation post. The reply came quickly.

"On roof of movie theater. Watching you walk now. Saw you with the boys. Assume I'm scoping red shirt?"

Keri responded just as fast.

"And anyone who approaches him."

Keri stepped inside the coffee shop and found a small window table where she sat restlessly, trying to look casual. She pretended to read the business section of the *LA Times*, while she was really focused on Woody in the red shirt standing a few feet from the chair. She glanced at her watch for the third time in the last three minutes. It was 1:28 p.m. The meet was supposed to happen in two minutes. She sent Castillo one last text.

"Going dark to stay focused. Keep me apprised."

At 1:30 p.m. exactly, Woody sat down. Since he didn't know what to do beyond that, he mostly looked around cluelessly, note in hand, waiting to be approached.

Keri scoured the area for anyone who looked even vaguely like the man who'd abducted Evie five years ago. But no one even came close.

Even with her sunglasses on, she made sure to look down at the paper intermittently. If the Collector had really come, he was probably scoping out everyone as well. She had no real expectations that the man who took her daughter would just walk up to Woody and say "Hi, I steal kids for a living. How may I help you?"

And if he was there, the Collector needed to know that his potential client, unless the person was an idiot, wouldn't actually sit in that chair. That's why she'd offered up Woody, with his head bopping around like a caffeinated squirrel. Even before he read her note, she was sending the Collector a message that his potential client was careful enough to send a sub.

After fifteen uneventful minutes, Woody got up and walked away, looking confused but generally happy. He'd just made $100 for sitting in a chair.

Keri's phone buzzed and she glanced at it. It was a text from Castillo:

"I've got nothing. No one approached. Was going to follow red shirt in case someone makes contact later. Cool?"

Keri typed back:

"Yes, thanks. Going to keep eyes on the chair. Keep me posted."

Keri sat there for another forty-five minutes, just in case. Finally, she gave up. As she prepared to leave, she called Castillo.

"Anything?" she asked.

"Nothing. He walked to some bar and met a few friends. He's been playing pool for the last twenty minutes. I'm sorry, Detective Locke."

"No, that's okay," Keri said, forcing down the catch in her throat. "It was always a long shot. Thanks anyway. I owe you one. And Castillo, please remember—"

"This is just between us," the young officer said, reading her mind. "Don't worry. My lips are sealed."

Keri hung up and returned to her car, typing out a quick e-mail to the Collector on the way back that said simply "where were you?"

It wasn't until she closed the door of the Prius and was cocooned in the silence of the parking garage that the full impact of the failure hit her. She'd known intellectually that the meet was unlikely to bear fruit but part of her had hoped anyway. Now that hope had been dashed.

Before she knew what was happening, she felt massive, chest-wracking sobs consume her. Her whole body shook, rattling her ribs, her shoulder, and everything else. But she couldn't stop it and she didn't care. She just gave in to the all-consuming pain, crying until there was no water left for tears.

And then she was driving, not even entirely sure where she was headed, letting her pain and her fury and her most primal instincts guide her wherever they wanted. When she finally stopped, she looked up to see where she was. It took a second to register but once she recognized the place, she knew why she had come here and what she had to do.

CHAPTER TWENTY THREE

Keri, raw with rage and numb to everything else, walked purposefully through the huge lobby atrium of the massive office tower where her ex-husband worked, ignoring the security guard who called after her. She punched the elevator button and waited impatiently.

She wasn't sure exactly what she was going to say to Stephen when she saw him. But she felt like she'd just had Evie ripped from her a second time. And despite their differences, he was the one person in the world who could understand what she was going through right now. And he might be the only one who could help.

Just as the elevator arrived, the guard caught up to her. He was a squat, doughy guy in his late twenties with a weak mustache and watery eyes.

"I'm sorry, ma'am. You'll have to sign in. Please come back to the security desk."

She stepped into the elevator without a word, flashed him her badge, and pushed the button for the forty-sixth floor. The guard was still squinting to read her ID when the doors closed on him.

The two women standing next to her, both in their fifties, could sense the fury emanating from her and inched uncomfortably to the far corner of the elevator. Neither made eye contact. Keri didn't care. When the doors opened at the seventeenth floor they scurried out as quickly as they could. Keri watched them go with mild amusement.

As she stepped out on the forty-sixth floor, she could tell that, despite showing her badge, security had already warned the receptionist about her arrival. The young woman looked barely old enough to vote. She stood up, partially blocking the fancy vanity logo for the company, ACA, or the Agency for Creative Artists.

"May I help you?" the girl asked, her voice wavering.

"Yes. I'm here to see my ex-husband, Stephen Locke. No need to buzz him. I know the way."

She started walking down the hallway of the Century City talent agency she hadn't visited since before she and Stephen got divorced. Since then, he'd gotten remarried to a young starlet, had a little boy with her, and been promoted to the head of the agency's TV department. But she knew he'd still have the same office as before. Stephen hated change.

The receptionist was trying desperately to keep up with her but had trouble because of her five-inch heels. By the time Keri got to Stephen's door, the poor girl was a good fifteen paces back.

Stephen was standing behind his desk, wearing a headset, talking quickly and animatedly waving his hands about. He looked much the same as the last time she'd see him, almost two years ago.

His longish, wavy brown hair fell casually across his face and he wore thin, stylish glasses. He looked trim and healthy and the bags he always had under his eyes when they were together were gone.

When he looked up and saw Keri, he froze for a moment before regaining his composure.

"I'm going to have to call you back," he said to whoever was on the other end of the line. Then he hung up and took off the headset.

The receptionist had finally caught up and stopped in the doorway next to Keri.

"I'm so sorry, Mr. Locke. She just stormed right by me."

"It's okay, Brandi," he said.

"Security is on their way up."

"That's all right. You can cancel that. Ms. Locke isn't a security risk. You can leave us be. Can you close the door behind us, please?"

"Yes sir," Brandi said and did as he asked as Keri stepped inside.

They looked at each other for a long second before speaking. Now that she was actually here, Keri wasn't sure how to begin.

"Keri, this is a surprise. I heard about your run-in with that guy who kidnapped the senator's daughter. You're looking pretty good considering I heard you were hospitalized for a while."

"Thanks," she said, ignoring the fact that he'd never even called to check on her. She needed to stay in control and resentment wouldn't help with that. "You're looking well."

"Thank you. I've turned into a bit of a CrossFit fanatic. What can I do for you?"

"I need your help, Stephen," she said, not wasting any time.

"With what?" he asked warily.

"I have a strong lead on the man I think took Evie. But I can't use department resources to go after him. So I need access to yours."

Keri watched Stephen take a moment to let it sink in.

"What do you mean? Why can't the department help?"

She could already tell he was getting his guard up. This wasn't going how she'd hoped it would go. She'd been in such a rush to get here that she hadn't thought through what to do next. Now she was committed. She'd have to be more forthcoming than she wanted.

"The methods I used to get the lead weren't totally legal," she admitted. "If I go to my lieutenant, I'll have to explain where I got the information. He won't be able to authorize it and I might get arrested myself."

"Jesus, Keri, what did you do?" he asked. His face had that same quizzical expression he wore so often when they were together. He'd seemed baffled by her through much of their marriage and apparently nothing had changed.

"I really can't say any more than I already have. You could get in trouble if you knew. But there's nothing wrong with you, as a private citizen, providing resources to investigate a lead. That's what I need from you—money and the willingness to use it."

"How would you use it?" he asked, clearly intrigued despite his apprehension.

"I'd hire a tech expert to do some digital searching. I'd also need a full-service investigative agency with human and surveillance resources, one with experience trailing subjects without being detected. I know of a couple of quality options."

Keri could tell that he was feeling overwhelmed. But Stephen got easily overwhelmed by most things that didn't involve making deals for his clients. And she didn't have time to hold his hand through this. She needed to get the process started soon. So, despite his obvious unease, she pressed on.

"In addition, I'd need walking around money I can pass out to people in the abduction underworld, people who might have useful information. And I'd need it all quick. My lead is time-sensitive. Twenty-four hours from now, it might go cold."

Stephen sat down at his desk and put his head in his hands. Keri wanted to shake him, to scream at him that he should be jumping at their first real chance to find their daughter's kidnapper.

Instead, she stood quietly, waiting for him to pull it together. Stephen had a habit of shutting down emotionally when things got bad. She hoped he could rein in that instinct this time.

After what felt like forever, he looked up at her. Studying his eyes, she knew his answer before he spoke.

"I'm sorry, Keri. But I just can't. I can't be involved in something that is so legally questionable."

"I'm not asking you to do anything legally questionable," she insisted. "I'm basically asking for a loan. It just so happens that it's a loan that could help find our daughter."

Stephen sighed deeply before responding.

"I know part of you believes that," he said. "And part of me wants to as well. But I think that deep down, you know the truth. Evie's never coming back. And the sooner you make your peace with that, the sooner you can start to heal."

Keri felt the anger start to bubble up inside her and tried to force it down.

If I blow up at him, he'll never help.

"Stephen, what will help me heal is getting our daughter back. Short of that, I'll even take knowing what really happened to her. Giving me this money can help me achieve that and it in no way impedes your 'healing.'"

She knew that last sarcastic line was counterproductive but she could feel her control starting to slip away. Stephen, as usual, remained impassive.

"Keri. You're obsessed. Think about what you're doing. You took a job that requires you to search for missing children. Every day you go into work and rip off the same scab over and over again. It's not good for you."

He said it with such bland aloofness that she wanted to punch him. She used to love how his cool reserve tempered her perpetual hot-headedness. But now, without Evie to smooth out the edges between them, she couldn't stand him. His emotionless condescension was too much to bear.

"Are you going to give me the money or not?" she asked one last time.

"I'm sorry, Keri."

Hearing that, the last vestiges of restraint disappeared and she let herself go, saying the words she'd wanted him to hear for years now.

"Yeah, I'm sorry too. I'm sorry that you care more about your reputation than your child. We both know that you aren't even sure you want Evie back. It would be too disruptive to your perfect world to have an emotionally damaged thirteen-year-old back in your life. It'd be too raw for you. After all, you're set, right? You've got your actress wife. You've got your little replacement child. How old is little Sammy now—two? And Shalene doesn't want to be a stepmom to a girl she's never met and who might require extra attention. It's all too messy, right, Stephen?"

There was a long, thick stretch of silence between them before Stephen finally spoke.

"I think you should go," he said.

"Yeah, I guess I should. No reason to stick around. But remember, when I find her, and I *will* find her, your daughter's going to ask what you did to help. And you'll have to explain to her that you didn't do a damn thing. And why? Because it was inconvenient."

She left, slamming the heavy door behind her so hard that a painting fell off the hallway wall, shattering the glass. She stormed back to reception where two security guards were waiting. When they saw her, both of them stepped aside without a word, letting her enter the elevator alone. The doors closed but Keri waited until it had starting going down before she began screaming in helpless fury.

CHAPTER TWENTY FOUR

Everything was fuzzy. Keri blinked several times, trying to drive the cloudiness from her eyes. Her mouth felt bone dry and her whole body ached. An annoying ringing in the distance seemed to be getting louder. She forced her eyes open and took in her surroundings.

She was on the houseboat, sprawled out on her stomach on the loveseat in her tiny living space. Her right arm and leg dangled off the side. When she tried to move them, she realized both were asleep.

Her head throbbed and she felt like she might throw up. And still, the ringing sound kept getting louder. Finally she realized what it was—her alarm clock. It was over by her bed, about six feet away, a seemingly insurmountable distance.

Then her phone began to chime too. It was lying on the coffee table, only three feet away. But that still felt like a hundred yards to her. She tried to shimmy over to it but lost her balance and fell off the love seat completely.

I don't think I've ever been this hung over in my entire life.

She managed to get a hand on the phone and turn off that alarm but the clock by the bed still seemed like an impossible journey. She rolled over onto her knees and used her elbows to push off the coffee table and reach something approximating a standing position.

She lurched over to the bed and punched the button on the clock, finally silencing it. Then she sat on the bed, trying to move as little as possible. She was tempted to lie down but something told her she shouldn't.

She looked at the clock. It read 7:15 a.m. Why had she set her alarm so early last night? She must have made the conscious choice to do it. But she couldn't recall the reason. Everything from the night before was mostly one big haze.

Flashes of detail from the evening came to her. Stopping at Ralph's to get some chicken wings and a fresh bottle of Glenlivet on the way home from her awful meeting with Stephen; watching one of the interchangeable series about the Kardashians while she downed the whole thing; throwing up.

Before she could piece together any more details, her phone rang. Realizing she'd left it on the coffee table, Keri used the wall to pull herself upright and lumbered back over to grab it.

"Hello," she said, not even looking at the caller ID.

"Keri, are you up?" The voice belonged to Detective Kevin Edgerton.

"Of course I'm up. Why are you calling to ask me that?"

"Because you told me to when you called last night."

"I did?"

"Yeah, you said you were going to get rip-roaring drunk and told me to call you this morning at seven fifteen to make sure you were up in time to get to the Burlingame update meeting at eight."

Oh shit—the meeting. How am I going to make myself presentable and get to the station by eight? Meanwhile, Edgerton thinks I'm crazy.

"That's right. It slipped my mind. Thanks, Kevin, although you're a little late. I have the time as seven eighteen."

"I know. I'm sorry about—"

"Don't sweat it," she said, pleased that she'd put him on the defensive. Hopefully, he wouldn't dwell on the whole drunk thing. "See you soon."

She hung up and stumbled toward the bathroom. The woman staring back at her in the mirror looked like a stranger—pale, blotchy skin, red eyes with dark circles under them, matted hair. She looked ten years older than her thirty-five years.

She grabbed a bag and quickly began stuffing it with what she'd need for the day—a change of clothes, her towel and shower toiletries, her gun belt, and a huge bottle of water. Then she hurried from the boat to the comfort station on the dock. The chill in the morning air both revived and annoyed her.

I've got to check out that apartment Ray mentioned. What adult woman has to walk a quarter mile to take a shower?

As she walked, Keri checked her phone. There were multiple texts and voice messages from yesterday, all of which she'd either ignored or missed. One text was from Ray in the late afternoon, asking why she never met up with Rene, the guy with the apartment to rent. Another text was from Stephen, pleading with her to get help.

Next up was a voicemail:

"Hi, Detective Locke. This is Susan Granger calling. I don't want to bother you. I know you got hurt a lot fighting that bad guy. But you promised you would come visit me when you got better and I was hoping you didn't forget. Anyway, thanks. Bye."

Keri hadn't thought she could feel any worse, what with the pounding headache, dehydration, nausea, sore ribs and shoulder, and self-disgust. But now she could add guilt to the ledger.

Susan Granger was a fourteen-year-old runaway who'd been forced into street prostitution by a pimp named Crabby. While investigating the disappearance of Ashley Penn two weeks ago, Keri had come across the two of them on a Venice street and briefly mistook Susan for what she imagined a teenage Evie would look like.

After beating up Crabby and getting him put away, she got Susan placed in a group home in Redondo Beach. They'd been in touch on the phone a few times but Keri had assured the girl she would visit when she felt better.

Somehow, the combination of her injuries and her reluctance to be face to face again with a girl who reminded her of Evie's possible fate had kept her away until now. But the disappointment in Susan's voice on the message told her she'd stalled far too long.

Keri got in the shower and tried to push the shame she felt away, focusing only on the soap and shampoo. It didn't work, as images of Susan, all tarted up and wearing a miniskirt on the street in the middle of the night, kept creeping into her head.

After getting dressed and throwing on a bit of makeup to hide her rough night, Keri booked it over to the station. She walked into Conference Room A at 7:58 a.m., with two minutes to spare. Even Lieutenant Hillman hadn't made it in yet. She sat down between Suarez and Edgerton and leaned over to the younger man.

"Thanks for this morning," she whispered. He nodded and smiled but didn't reply as Hillman had just entered the room.

"Okay," he said without any opening pleasantries. "I understand we've got some updates this morning. Who's first?"

Garrett Patterson raised his hand and Hillman motioned for him to come to the front of the room. Patterson stepped forward and turned on the big computer monitor screen that dominated the back wall.

"So, we know that Kendra's individual checking account was emptied and that a ticket was purchased in Palm Springs by someone who looked like her under the name A. Maroney, which fits with her middle initial and maiden name. The ticket was for a bus to Phoenix but there is no evidence of the woman getting off there. But we now think we do know where she got off."

"Where?" Brody asked impatiently.

"Blythe, California, just west of the Arizona border," Patterson said, as the monitor displayed a receipt on the screen. "We have a record of a car being rented down the street from the bus station. The name on the credit card was A. Maroney. The car was turned in yesterday morning in El Paso, Texas."

"Great," Brody grumbled. "She could have walked across the border into Mexico from there and we'd never know where she went after that."

"Actually, we think that's exactly what she did. But we didn't lose her. Right, Manny?"

Detective Manny Suarez took that as his cue and stood up next to Patterson.

"Being the only bilingual member of this unit, I volunteered to get in touch with the Mexican authorities. Eventually I was put in touch with the right folks and they sent me this."

The screen was replaced with a printout of what looked like an airplane manifest. Suarez continued.

"This is a record of a flight from Juarez to Mexico City yesterday. Notice the seventeenth name on the manifest—A. Maroney. And here's surveillance footage from the gate area as people boarded the flight."

Keri looked at the grainy images. After a few moments she saw what looked like the woman from the Palm Springs bus station. She was wearing a different outfit but had the same headscarf and sunglasses and was careful to keep her head down the whole time.

Suarez put a new image on the screen.

"This is a record of a different flight," he said. "This one is from yesterday late afternoon. It went from Mexico City to Barcelona."

"Barcelona, Spain?" Cantwell asked, stunned.

"Yep," Suarez answered. "Here's footage of the same woman boarding that flight. And this image is from early this morning at the Barcelona airport."

On the screen were several screen captures of what looked like the same woman. One was of her leaving the gate after getting off the plane. Another was of her walking down a concourse. And the last image was of her waiting in line at a bus stop outside the airport departure area.

"That's the last shot of her we have of her. Buses do pickups there every ten minutes and stop throughout the city. There's no way to track her after that."

"And there's something else," Edgerton added, piping up for the first time. "Manny, can you go to the cleaned up shot from the bus station waiting area?"

As Suarez looked for the image, Edgerton turned to Keri.

"Do you remember how you asked us to clean up the footage of her reading that magazine in the station? Well, we did and this is what we found."

On the screen appeared a close-up of the woman holding the magazine. The title was a little fuzzy but Keri could make it out. It was called *Living Spain*.

"Well, I'd say that seals it," Brody announced triumphantly.

"What about the prints from the snow globe?" Keri asked.

Edgerton shook his head.

"Palm Springs PD is still going through them. They've identified fourteen prints definitively but nothing from Kendra yet. They're still processing others but they told me that even with her touching it, they might not be able to get a clean print. Just too many fingers on the things."

Lieutenant Hillman looked at Keri. She knew he was waiting on her since she was always the last one to want to close out a case. That instinct had served her well when everyone else had assumed Ashley Penn had run away. She had doggedly stayed with that case against direct orders and was eventually proven right. A teenage girl was alive because of her stubbornness.

But despite her gut feeling that something was off, she couldn't think of anything concrete that could justify not closing the case.

"Her sister told me she was fluent in Spanish," she said reluctantly. "So it makes sense that if she wanted to get away, she'd go to a place where she knew the language. It all fits."

"I agree," Hillman said, stepping forward. "Here's how this is going to work, folks. We're not going to officially close the case yet. It's only been seventy-two hours since she's gone missing. Something might still turn up. And besides, the husband will raise a stink if we tell him we're closing it out. This woman is the closest thing to a saint we've got in this city and we don't need Burlingame going to the press, saying we've abandoned his wife. But for all practical purposes, we're closing it out. Move on to your other cases. If anything pops on this one, we'll revisit it. Understood?"

Everyone nodded their assent.

"And Locke," he added, "take the rest of the day off. I think we pushed you back in the field too early. You look like death warmed over. Get a good night's sleep and we'll see you tomorrow."

"Yes sir," Keri said. For the first time in a long time she didn't feel like fighting him. All she wanted was to go home and sleep. She headed out of the station, checking for any messages she might have missed during the meeting. There was one e-mail waiting for her.

It was from the Collector.

CHAPTER TWENTY FIVE

In shock and suddenly feeling weak-kneed, she reached out for the closest wall to keep from falling.

The message was in response to her e-mail from yesterday afternoon asking "where were you?"

His reply was short and to the point:

i was there. you were not. caution is good. you passed that test. but trust is key. maybe next time.

Keri got in her car, closed the door, and sat quietly, not moving. She couldn't decide if the message was crushing or hopeful. He hadn't ended the communication completely. He'd even hinted that a next time was possible.

But she had no idea how to ensure that possibility without risking scaring him off. Finally she decided, in violation of the very essence of her character, to do nothing, at least for now.

I'm tired. I'm hung over. I feel sick. I'm physically hurt. And I'm stressed beyond belief. This isn't the time to reach out and risk making a mistake. Just let it go.

With the decision made, Keri felt a weight suddenly lift. She still felt like crap. But at least she could move forward. At least she could function. At least she could focus on other tasks without feeling like a raw, throbbing nerve every second. And she knew the task she needed to focus on at this moment.

*

As she pulled up in front of the group home in North Redondo Beach, Keri hung up the phone. She'd just finished leaving what she hoped was a gracious message for Randall the GameStop employee.

For some reason she was in a generous mood and he was the beneficiary. She thanked him for his help yesterday and said that while he was cute and sweet, she'd decided to get back together with her boyfriend. Feeling proud of herself for the first time all day, Keri got out of the car and headed for the house.

To the average person the South Bay Shared House looked like any other home in the neighborhood. It sat back from the street, surrounded by thick palm trees, and the Mediterranean-style design fit in with the surrounding residences.

The only signs that the place was any different were the unusually high stone walls that surrounded the house and the unobtrusively placed cameras that stared out at the sidewalk and street in both directions.

They were an unfortunate necessity as many of the residents, all teenage girls, were victims of domestic violence. On rare occasions the perpetrator discovered the house's address and tried to make an unannounced visit.

Keri rang the bell at the exterior gate and waited for someone to respond. She could tell there was a camera trained on her as well and she held up her badge and ID to make things easier for whoever was checking her out. After a moment, a voice came over the intercom.

"How can I help you, Detective?" asked a raspy-voiced woman.

"I'm Keri Locke, here to see Susan Granger. She requested a visit."

"We normally ask that visitors make prior arrangements, Detective Locke."

"I understand. But I've been incapacitated for a while. This is the first chance I've really had to come by. Can you make an exception?"

There was a long silence. Then Keri heard a buzz. She pulled the gate door open and walked to the front door, where a tiny woman waited for her. She had thick glasses and her gray hair was tied up in a bun. Her powerfully wrinkled skin suggested a lifetime of smoking and too much sun.

"Incapacitated for a while," she said as Keri approached, sounding like she was mildly amused. "That's one way of putting it. I saw you on the news, Detective. I'm surprised you're walking already. I would have thought you'd be in a wheelchair for a month."

"Yeah, well. They got sick of me at the hospital so they kicked me out. I figured if they were willing to let me leave on my own two feet, I should try to stay upright on them."

The woman started to laugh but it quickly turned into a long, hacky cough. Oblivious, she waved for Keri to follow her in. When she recovered, she closed the door and proceeded to secure the three separate locks on it.

"Susan will be happy to see you," she said as they walked down a long hallway decorated with intricate ceramic tile flooring. "I'm Rita Skraeling, by the way. I run the place. Call me Rita."

"Hi, Rita, call me Keri. How's she doing?"

"Good days and bad. Therapy sessions have been tough this week. But she's really trying. And the other girls have taken her under their wing. A lot of them know what she's been through so they can relate."

"How many girls do you have here?"

"It varies, usually between four and eight. Right now we have five with Susan. She's in the library."

They rounded the corner and Keri saw that the library was just a sun room with two full bookshelves. There was a loveseat by the window and two beanbag chairs, one of which Susan occupied. She was casually reading a Nancy Drew mystery.

She looked shockingly different from the one and only time Keri had seen her on that Venice street. That night she could have passed for nineteen or twenty. But now, wearing sweatpants and a navy-blue T-shirt, free of makeup, with her blonde hair in a loose ponytail and her legs curled up under her, she looked closer to twelve.

Susan sensed eyes on her and looked up fearfully. But the second she saw Keri, she softened and her face broke into a wide smile. She clambered to her feet and ran over, hugging her tight. Keri winced but forced herself not to grunt as her ribs were crushed.

"Careful, Ms. Granger. Remember, Detective Locke is still recovering from her injuries."

Susan immediately pulled back.

"Sorry. I forgot," she said quietly.

"That's okay," Keri assured her and lifted her arms like a bodybuilder showing off his muscles. "Strong like bull."

Susan giggled.

"I'll leave you two be," Rita said and left without another word.

"Want to sit down?" Keri asked. Susan nodded shyly and they sat down on the loveseat.

"Thanks for coming."

"Of course. I'm sorry it took me so long," Keri said, deciding not to explain beyond that.

"That's okay. I know you've had a lot going on. I just wanted to make sure you didn't forget."

Keri ignored the fresh wave of guilt that washed over her.

"No, of course not," she said reassuringly. "So how are things here?"

"Pretty good. Ms. Skraeling's tough—but in a good way. The girls are nice. Mostly I just like being able to be awake in the day and sleep at night."

Keri nodded, trying to ignore the catch in her own throat. She remembered that this girl had spent almost every night of the last few years walking the streets, satisfying the grotesque urges of men three and four times her age. The thought made her want to cry, gag, and punch someone all at the same time.

"That's good," she managed to say with an even voice.

"How's the other girl doing, the one who was taken—Ashley?" Susan asked.

"Oh wow. I haven't had a chance to check in on her either. She was hurt pretty badly, especially her leg. But I know she was recovering well physically. The doctors said she'd even be able to surf again at some point. I should really go see her too. Maybe I'll do that later today."

"I worry about her," Susan said with a sincerity that took Keri's breath away.

"I do too, sweetie," she said. "But she's like you, tough. She'll be okay."

"Speaking of tough, you promised me you'd teach me some of that Krav Maga stuff you used to take down Crabby. I know you're too sore right now. But when you're feeling better, do you think you could come back and show me some moves?"

"You bet. But for now, I think couch time is the way to go."

Susan laughed again, giving Keri a jolt of energy that seemed to make her aches and pains fade, at least for a moment. The girl looked at her shyly before working up the courage to ask the question that had obviously been in the back of her head.

"When did you decide to become a detective?"

"Ah, I see you're reading Nancy Drew. Got detectives on the brain, huh?"

Susan didn't answer but waited quietly. She wanted a real answer and wouldn't be diverted. Keri decided to respect her enough to give her the truth.

"Well, it was a few years ago. I was a professor who taught about crime and criminals. One day in the park my daughter was abducted, right in front of me. I felt so helpless. And I really fell apart for a while after that. To be honest, I'm still not all put back together. I lost my job. My marriage broke up. But a detective friend of mine convinced me that with my experience, I might make a good detective myself. And I started to think that he might be right. I thought that it might be a way to help other people in trouble, even if I couldn't help my own little girl. So that's what I try to do now. Help people, especially missing people, find their way back home."

She finished speaking. Susan took her hand and squeezed it. Neither of them spoke for a long time. Finally, Susan broke the silence.

"I think you should come to visit me a lot. I don't want you to be lonely." Her voice was full of genuine concern. Keri didn't know whether to chuckle or cry.

"How about this?" she replied. "Why don't we make this a weekly thing? With this job, I can't make too many promises. But I'll try to visit every week to discuss whatever you like. We could even turn it into a Nancy Drew book club. I'll read the same one as you and we can talk about it when I come by next. What do you think?"

Susan nodded, holding up the book title so Keri could write it down. It was called *The Secret of the Old Clock*.

Then the girl got quiet again, as if lost in thought.

"What is it, sweetie?" Keri asked. "Are you okay?"

After several more seconds, Susan looked up at her and spoke with great solemnity.

"I think I'd like to be a detective one day too," she said.

"I have a feeling you'd be a great one."

CHAPTER TWENTY SIX

Keri was so lost in thought that she barely noticed the freeway signs or the traffic around her as she headed back from Redondo Beach. Then something seemed to suddenly click inside her, like she'd been in hibernation until now and had only just woken up.

Instead of getting off the 405 freeway and returning to the houseboat, she continued north. Her conversation with Susan had reminded her of something.

No matter how screwed up my own life is, I am good at what I do for a living because I care. I fight for those who can't fight for themselves. That's what I do. And that's what I'm going to do for Kendra Burlingame.

Something had been eating at Keri, nibbling at the edges of her brain. But she'd been ignoring it because it didn't seem worth pursuing. But that's what she did—pursued leads wherever they took her. And that's what she would do now.

Twenty minutes later, she arrived at an unimpressive-looking three-story building in Culver City, literally thirty feet from the freeway. It housed Los Angeles's best known alternative weekly newspaper, *Weekly LA*. It was also, much to Keri's surprise, the workplace of Margaret "Mags" Merrywether.

Keri checked in at reception and was met in less than a minute by Mags herself. She wasn't wearing an evening gown this time, but even her regular work clothes were stunning. She wore a loose cream blouse unbuttoned well past where Keri felt comfortable, fitted black slacks, and a pair of heeled sandals that clomped loudly as she walked. Her flaming red hair was pulled up into a messy but somehow still elegant bun.

"This is a magnificently unexpected surprise," she said, a broad smile on her face.

"Hi, Mags. It's good to see you. You mind if we talk privately?"

"Of course not. Is this a 'go down the street to the coffee shop' chat or a 'closed office door' discussion?"

"The latter, I think."

"Oh dear. Well, come on back then."

She led the way down the hallway, seamlessly navigating the boxes piled everywhere and the occasional stray desk or chair. Eventually they arrived at an office only slightly larger than Keri's galley with a view of cars zipping by, dangerously close, on the freeway. It was packed to the gills with stacks of neatly organized papers piled high. Every bookshelf was full. The walls were covered with photos and framed front pages of the paper.

"Please excuse the mess. I'd like to say it's unusual. But it's not. Have a seat."

Keri closed the door behind her and maneuvered herself into the small wooden chair in front of Mags's desk.

"What exactly do you do here?" she asked.

"I write a column under the name 'Mary Brady.'"

"That's the muckraking column—the one that got the deputy mayor indicted and exposed the payoffs in the sanitation department. That's you?"

"Guilty as charged," Mags said, her eyes gleaming with delight.

"Based on the other evening, I wouldn't have taken you for a 'power to the people' ink-stained, shoe leather type."

"Yes, well, I guess we're all full of secrets, aren't we? So what's up, Detective? Have you made any progress in finding Kenny?"

"Almost none. Despite what everyone she knows says, everything suggests she left town of her own accord. In fact, my being here would probably annoy my boss, since he probably rightly thinks the case is ready to be closed."

"And yet, here you are," Mags noted.

"That's right. I was talking with Kendra's sister yesterday—"

"Oh yes, Catherine. A woman of pure contentedness if ever I met one," Mags said in a tone that could be interpreted as both insult and compliment.

"Yes, well, she said something that I haven't been able to get out of my head."

"What's that?"

"She suggested that Kenny might have gotten a little bored with her life as Mrs. Jeremy Burlingame. She didn't know just where that boredom might lead, but said that you might, as you and Kenny were closer than the two of them these days. So is there anything to that? Did Kenny's boredom ever send her down an unexpected path?"

"Ah, Catherine, always chafing at being seen as the less principled Maroney sister. How clever of her to hint that Kenny might not be as proper as everyone thinks without saying it outright. Impressively passive-aggressive, don't you think?"

Keri stared hard at Mags. She liked her, probably more than she should like someone she was questioning. She could imagine how fun it would be to have a friend like Margaret Merrywether. The woman was like a modern-day Dorothy Parker.

But it was dangerous to get sucked in too much by the charm of any interview subject. It made it easy to miss things. And she got the distinct sense that Mags was trying to snow her.

"You know, Mags, I noticed that amid all those linguistic flourishes, you never answered my question."

"Didn't I?"

"Well, maybe I missed it amid all the 'passive-aggressive' psychobabble. So let me ask you a little more directly. To your knowledge, was Kendra Burlingame having an affair?"

"Oh my, so all our cards are being laid on the table, are they?"

Keri didn't answer, refusing to let Mags talk her way out of this one. Finally, she dropped her head and let out a big sigh. When she looked up again, the playfulness had left her eyes.

"Detective Locke, do you recall how I shared the information about Kenny's photo shoot with you on the condition that you keep it quiet if at all possible?"

"I do. And I believe I honored that request."

"I'm going to make the same request of you again. Will you agree to it?"

"As long as what you tell me ends up not being relevant to the case, I'll do my best. But I can't make any promises."

"I understand. And as before, your word is good enough for me. Five years ago, Kenny learned that she couldn't have children. She took it hard at first. But eventually she started thinking about adoption or a surrogate. Unfortunately, Jeremy wasn't interested in being a parent, no matter how the child came their way. He said it would be too disruptive. She decided that if they weren't both committed to the idea, then it wasn't a wise choice. But she was unhappy. I'd go so far as to say depressed."

"Did she take anything for it?"

"She did. And I think it helped. But she was still a bit lost. And I think she resented Jeremy a bit too. It was right around that time that she met a man in her yoga class."

"What's his name?"

"Alex Crane. She told me he's an illustrator for children's books, very in touch with his emotions—the antithesis of Jeremy. And he's a little younger. When they met, Kenny was thirty-three and I think he was in his late twenties. Also apparently he's gorgeous and buff and you know, all of it."

Keri nodded. She knew the type. Mags continued.

"Anyway, they started out just talking, getting coffee after class. And extremely long story short, she ended up having a brief fling with him, maybe six weeks. I'm not even sure she enjoyed it, she felt so guilty. We'd talk and she'd just torture herself. She was betraying her husband, her principles, her very perception of who she was as a person. Anyway, she stopped it."

"How did Alex react?"

"Not especially well. I think he'd fallen in love with her. I mean, could you blame him? He called her and tried to see her a few times. But eventually he got the message and moved on. I know he's married now and has a baby."

"Did Kendra ever say that she was worried he might be dangerous?"

"She never used that word. She called him passionate. Sometimes I think she meant more than that though."

"Do you think Jeremy ever found out?"

"I never saw any indication of that. She considered telling him, just coming clean. But she worried it would hurt him too much and that he wouldn't look at her the same way afterward. Plus, she decided that telling him would be just a way to lessen her guilt. It wouldn't be for him."

"She was probably right," Keri said, speaking from painful personal experience.

"To be honest, I think Jeremy was oblivious to even the possibility that she might do something like that. I'm not even sure he knew she was taking yoga classes. He's so in his own world much of the time, focused on his work, that I think he just doesn't notice details like that."

"Okay, Mags. Thanks for this. Is there anything else I should know about Kenny? Now's the time to tell me. I won't be so accommodating if you hold back again."

"That's it, Detective. Kenny is a good person. She's made some bad choices, but not many. And she beats herself up for them more than anyone I know. I just don't want her good name dragged through the mud."

"I understand. But my priority is protecting her life. Her good name is secondary."

"Of course. It's just…it's hard to find really good friends out here. And Kendra is a great friend. The thought that she might be gone…" Mags trailed off.

For the first time, Keri saw real emotion behind the tough-broad façade.

"I'll do my best for her," Keri promised.

Mags nodded, grabbed a tissue, and dabbed at what almost looked like a tear.

"So now that we've completed the 'closed door' part of your visit," she said, regaining her composure, "did you want to join me for that coffee?"

"I actually would. But I can't right now. I've got to be somewhere."

"Somewhere exciting, I hope?"

"I guess it depends. Do you consider interrogating buff, yoga-loving, kids' book–illustrating home wreckers exciting?"

"I do actually," Mags said.

"Yeah, so do I."

CHAPTER TWENTY SEVEN

Keri was a little ashamed of the anticipation she felt as she knocked on Alex Crane's apartment door. But her salacious curiosity about the man who'd made Kendra Burlingame stray had gotten the better of her.

Unfortunately, Alex wasn't as exciting as Keri expected. When he opened the door to his Mar Vista apartment, he was paunchier and balder than she'd anticipated. He wore loose jeans and an extra large maroon T-shirt. Keri could hear a baby squealing unhappily in the background and a female voice trying to soothe the little one.

"Can I help you?" he asked

"I think so. My name's Keri Locke. I'm a detective with LAPD Missing Persons. I need to talk to you about Kendra Burlingame."

Crane's expression turned panicky and he quickly looked over his shoulder to see if his wife was close by.

"Do we have to do this now?" he whispered.

"Who is it?" his wife called from another room.

"I'm afraid we do," Keri told him firmly.

"It's no one," Crane shouted back over his shoulder. "Just some woman whose car battery died. She's asking if I can give her a jump. I'll be right back."

"Please hurry, Alex," his wife called back. "I could really use some help here."

"I'll be quick," he answered as he grabbed his car keys and stepped outside. He silently led Keri out of the complex and down to the street, where he actually opened his trunk and started to reach for jumper cables. Keri noticed a crowbar suspiciously close and her right hand automatically went to her holster.

"Stop, Mr. Crane. Remove your hand from the trunk and close it."

"But if my wife comes out, I need to have these with me."

"I don't give a damn about your charade for your wife. Your hand is very close to something I consider a weapon right now. Pull it away, close the trunk, and sit down on the curb—now."

Crane did as he was told. After he sat down he looked up at her.

"I wondered if someone would be paying me a visit."

"You could have come to us."

"Come on. I have a wife and child. I haven't seen Kendra in years. I didn't see any point in dredging up old news for no good reason."

"The point is, now you look suspicious, Alex. If you'd come forward, you might have earned a few brownie points. Now I have to tear your life apart."

"Please—I had nothing to do with this. I'll answer all your questions."

"All right, let's start with where you were on Monday morning."

The flustered look on his face was almost immediately replaced with one of relief.

"Is that when she disappeared? That's great."

"That's great?" Keri asked angrily.

"Wait, that's not what I meant. It's just I was out of town then. I was on a work retreat in Ojai from Sunday through yesterday. There were at least a dozen people there the whole time. I was in like, fifteen meetings. Plus, I shared a hotel room with a co-worker. I can account for every second."

"What job was the retreat for?" Keri demanded, ignoring the sinking feeling that suddenly consumed her. "I thought you illustrated children's books."

"I used to. But it didn't pay enough. So I got a job as a technical illustrator. I draw the pictures for the instructions you get when you buy cabinets and desks and stuff."

"Really?"

"I got married and had a kid. I needed something steady, okay? It sucks obviously. I mean, what instructional manual company requires weekend retreats, right? But it pays. And it's where I was. So am I cleared?"

Keri looked at him, sitting slackly on the curb, and suspected that he probably was. Alex Crane was pathetic and self-involved. But she couldn't bring herself to buy that he was a lust-fueled abductor. He didn't look like he had the energy for it.

"If your alibi pans out, you'll be fine. But you need to help yourself, Alex."

"What do I have to do?" he asked eagerly.

"Call Detective Manny Suarez at this number," she said, handing him a card. "Tell him you spoke to me and that you're making a statement. Tell him everything—the affair, the Ojai trip, and anything else he wants to know. Do it now. Got it?"

He nodded and pulled out his phone right then. Keri left him sitting there and headed back to her car.

Crane may not be my man but there's still someone else who might be. Unfortunately, to find out for sure, I'm going to have to break that promise to Mags.

Jeremy Burlingame's Marina del Rey medical practice was in a twenty-story glass tower within walking distance of Keri's houseboat. She'd driven by it countless times without ever really noticing it. But now, as she rode up in the glass-sided elevator, she marveled at the view of the entire marina. Even her piddling little place, just a dot in the distance, looked respectable from this height.

The door opened and she stepped out into a sterile blue-and-gray-walled office with a vaulted ceiling and a view of the city. A receptionist smiled at her as she walked over.

"My name's Keri Locke. I have an appointment with Dr. Burlingame at two p.m."

"Okay, Ms. Locke," she said pleasantly, "if you could just fill out these forms and let me make a copy of your insurance card and driver's license, we'll be right with you."

"Oh, it's not that kind of appointment. I'm Detective Keri Locke, here about his wife. We spoke earlier and he said he'd fit me in."

"So sorry about that, Ms. Locke. I do see the note in the computer here. That's my fault," she said, sounding far more mortified than Keri thought was necessary. "Give me one moment and we'll get you right back there."

Keri walked around the reception area while she waited, looking at the framed images on the wall. Most of them were of smiling children, apparently happy success stories. A few others were of women in what looked like actor head shot pictures. Those all had the word "Butterfly" printed in the lower right corner of the photo. Keri had no idea what that meant.

A nurse opened the door and beckoned for Keri to follow her. They went down a long hall and around a bend to a large office in the northwest corner. The nurse knocked on the open door to get the attention of Burlingame, who was hunched over a file.

He looked up, slightly startled, then recovered and waved her in.

"Thanks for coming here, Detective. I wanted to see you as soon you called and I figured this was more convenient for both of us, logistically. Truth be told, I have appointments lined up until seven tonight so this works much better for me."

"Not a problem, Dr. Burlingame. Thanks for making the time. I just wanted to touch base with you about the case."

"Yes, thank you. I keep checking in with Lieutenant Hillman, but he never has anything to share. He mentioned that the investigation so far suggests she just left. I've told him repeatedly that that's not possible. I'm starting to worry that he's made up his mind and that Kendra's case isn't the priority for him that it is for me."

"Definitely not so, Doctor. We're still pursuing every available lead aggressively. In fact, I was interviewing someone of interest just before I came over here. Let me ask you, does the name Alex Crane mean anything to you?"

She watched him closely but Burlingame just looked mildly perplexed.

"I don't think so. If he was a patient I'd remember. Is he a witness or a suspect or something?"

"At this point, neither. What he was, at least for a time, was your wife's lover. Were you aware that Kendra was having an affair, Dr. Burlingame?"

The doctor's eyes widened in shock and disbelief.

"What?" he stammered. "What are you saying?"

"Your wife had an affair with a man named Alex Crane. Did you know that?" she asked more harshly this time.

"No, I mean, no, that's not true. It can't possibly be. This man, he must be lying—you know, fifteen minutes of fame. Please, you can't believe this. Kendra would never do that."

Keri didn't respond at first. All her attention was focused on Burlingame's face, looking for any hint of deception. She didn't know him well at all so she didn't have much to compare his reaction to. But he seemed genuinely distressed.

The cool reserve with which he normally carried himself was gone. He looked like a little boy who'd been separated from his mom in a big crowd and was now desperately searching for her.

"She never mentioned anything about this to you?"

"No, never. Are you saying she ran off with this man? Is that why Hillman won't be straight with me? I can't believe any of this."

"The affair occurred five years ago. It's been over for a long time, Doctor. She hasn't seen Crane since it ended."

"Wait, what? Then why are you telling me this? What good will it do?"

Keri watched the wheels turn in his head. He looked down at the desk, then back up at her, trying to control his rapid breathing. She could tell he'd figured it out.

"You thought I might have known about this man," he finally said, "that I might have done something to Kendra as payback. You wanted to see how I'd react when you told me."

"Yes," Keri said.

"And do you think I did something?"

"I honestly don't know, Doctor."

That wasn't exactly true. Nothing Jeremy Burlingame had said or done had given her reason to suspect him. The only mark against him was that he was her husband. And husbands are always suspects.

"Well, what can I do to prove to you that I didn't?" he pleaded. "Can I take a lie detector test? Do you want to take my phone to check my location the last few days? Do you want to interrogate the doctors I worked with in San Diego on Monday some more? What can I do to assure you of my innocence and keep you looking for her?"

There was a hint of desperation in his voice, as if he might lose it at any moment. But Keri had to keep pushing. It was her job.

"I'm not sure there's anything you can do, Dr. Burlingame. After all, it's almost always the husband. So you've got to expect that you'd be under suspicion."

"Yes, but I figured a good detective would follow the facts and not just make lazy assumptions based on clichés. I didn't expect you to walk in here and use allegations of an affair to test me. An affair, by the way, I think you may have just made up."

There was a knock on the door. A nurse stood meekly at the threshold.

"What is it, Brenda?" Burlingame demanded harshly.

"I'm sorry, Doctor. But Mrs. Rossetti has been waiting for twenty minutes and she's getting upset."

"I'll be right there," he said brusquely.

"Yes sir," Brenda said, backing away meekly.

He looked back at Keri, clearly frustrated.

"Are we done here, Detective? Or are you going to arrest me?"

"You're free to resume your schedule, Doctor."

"Let me ask you this, Detective Locke. Is there any legal reason why I can't hire my own private investigator to pursue this? I mean clearly, the police aren't interested. And despite what you may believe, I love my wife. Hell, I've been sleeping on the couch because I can't bear to lie in our bed without her beside me. I feel completely helpless."

"You're free to do as you wish, Doctor," Keri said, trying to keep her voice cool and professional. "But I can assure you, I'm still very much interested in this case." With that, she got up and left.

It wasn't until she got into the elevator that Keri allowed herself to breathe normally. She had just taken a huge risk. She'd conducted an aggressive interview with the missing woman's spouse, without the permission or even awareness of her superior.

And what did she have to show for it? Nothing. She was no more convinced of his guilt now than when she walked into his office. In fact, the sense of panic and powerlessness he projected made her feel like he was as much a victim as Kendra.

As the elevator plummeted to the ground floor, she couldn't help but wonder if her career was headed in the same direction.

CHAPTER TWENTY EIGHT

With a pit of apprehension in her gut, Keri drove from Burlingame's office to visit Ashley Penn in Venice. She was almost there when she got the call she'd been dreading. She hit the speakerphone button and braced for what she knew was coming.

"What the hell were you thinking?" bellowed the furious voice of Lieutenant Cole Hillman.

"Good afternoon, Lieutenant," she said as pleasantly as she could, "I'm not sure what you're referring to."

"I'm referring to you invading Burlingame's office and treating him like he's suspect number one when we all know there is no suspect."

"With all due respect, sir, you yourself said the case wasn't officially closed. I was just following up."

There was a long pause. Keri braced herself for another explosion.

"Locke, I thought I told you to go home and rest. Why can't you just follow orders for once, especially when they're for your own good?" He sounded less angry than pleading now.

"I just want to do the job right, Lieutenant."

"I get that. And I know you're itching to get back in the game. But part of your job is listening to your superior officer."

"Yes sir."

"So hear me now. You are to stop investigating this case. Go home. Sleep. Watch TV. Eat food that's bad for you. I don't care what you do, as long as it doesn't involve pursuing this nearly closed case. Are we clear?"

"Yes, sir. I just—"

"Good," he said, cutting her off and hanging up before she could get in another word.

Keri pulled the car over. She was parked on the street near Ashley Penn's house in the Venice canals. She had been ordered to drop the case, to go home.

Actually, he said he didn't care what I did as long as it wasn't pursuing the case. Checking up on a girl I rescued from certain death isn't pursuing the case.

Satisfied that she was following the letter of Hillman's orders, Keri got out of the car and walked to the Penn house.

The home of Senator Stafford Penn, his wife, Mia, and their daughter, Ashley, was a massive, three-story mansion surrounded by high walls and situated next to a canal modeled after those in the

Italian city. Keri buzzed the outer door and waved at the camera looking down at her.

After a few seconds, the gate buzzed and she walked toward the front door, which opened suddenly to reveal Ashley Penn. The fifteen-year-old girl stood in the doorway, supported by crutches, with an enormous cast on her right leg from ankle to hip. Her left wrist was wrapped in a soft cast.

Despite that, she wore a huge grin. Her blonde hair fell loosely over her shoulders. She had on a white tank top and navy shorts, both of which contrasted with her deeply tanned skin. Before Keri could stop her, the girl hobbled toward her, dropped the crutches, and wrapped her arms around her, giving her a powerful hug. Keri didn't mind the ripple of pain that shot through her.

"It's so good to see you," Ashley whispered in her ear. When she finally stepped back, there were tears in her eyes. Keri's were wet too.

"You look pretty good, considering," Keri said and meant it. From the waist up, the teenage girl looked like she was ready for a modeling shoot. She picked up the crutches and returned them.

"Thanks," Ashley said as she led Keri into the house. "So do you. The last time I saw you, you were in a wheelchair with your arm in a sling. Now you're dressed all professional woman–like. I'd never know you were in a hospital like, a week ago."

"I look better than I feel, trust me."

They sat down in the front sitting room. It was a little formal but Ashley obviously couldn't go long distances and this room had the closest couch. A maid came in and asked if they needed anything. Ashley asked for lemonade and Keri followed suit. A tall, solid-looking man in a crisp suit stood just outside the room, silent but alert. Keri recognized him as part of Senator Penn's security staff.

"Is this just a social visit or is it related to the case?" Ashley asked, a hint of apprehension in her voice.

I just wanted to check in, see how you were doing," Keri assured her. "I felt bad that I hadn't had a chance to stop by yet."

"Don't feel bad. It's probably better that you waited anyway. Things have been a little crazy around here."

"What do you mean?"

"My folks are separating. Dad moved out over the weekend. He's issuing a statement tomorrow to try to beat the tabloids to it."

"I'm sorry to hear that, Ashley."

"It's okay. It's been coming. My mom hasn't been happy for a while. Me getting kidnapped by a guy who was hired by my father's

142

brother didn't help. And my dad trying to keep it all quiet because it would hurt his reelection chances was just sort of the cherry on top."

"I wish I could say I was stunned. But I have to admit, your father didn't seem to love it when things went…off-script."

"That's a nice way of putting it. Look, I love him. He's my dad. But family is not his top priority. It sometimes felt like we were an obstacle to his perfect little life. He's kind of a control freak, you know?"

"Don't you think that's a bit harsh?" Keri asked.

"No way. When things don't go how he planned, he just kind of loses it. He's learned to control it because he's a politician and voters don't like rage monsters. But when things don't go his way, especially when he thinks he's been wronged, he seethes to himself. And eventually, it comes out later."

"Through violence? He hasn't hurt you or your mother, has he?" Keri asked, alarmed.

"No. He's not violent. But I remember that in his last election, some local councilman endorsed his primary opponent after privately promising my dad he'd support him. Within a year, the guy had lost his seat, his home had been foreclosed on, and he was being investigated by the city attorney."

"Well, if the guy was corrupt—"

"He wasn't. It was all bogus. But by the time the truth came out, his life had been destroyed. Then there was this rich Malibu socialite who reneged on hosting a campaign fundraiser at the last minute. My dad got her kicked out of her country club. He had her investigated for a zoning violation. That ended up being false too. But by then, she'd been shamed into moving. She lives in La Jolla now. I could tell you a dozen other stories like that. He's not a great guy."

"I'm sorry," Keri said, unsure what else she could add.

"Me too. It's just good my mom knows all this stuff too or he'd probably try to crush her in the divorce. But he can't because she knows where all the bodies are buried."

Their lemonade arrived and Keri used the distraction as a chance to change the subject.

"When do you go back to school?" she asked.

"Next week. I'm a little nervous. All that publicity—I'm not sure how people are going to react."

"Your friends have come to visit you, right? Have they acted any differently toward you?"

"No, they've been awesome. Someone's been by every day to bring me homework and just hang out." Ashley smiled at the thought of it.

"See, the people who matter have already shown their true colors," Keri said, then leaned in to whisper her next comment. "I say screw anyone who doesn't get with the program."

Ashley nodded but Keri could tell she wasn't totally convinced. She decided not to push.

"Have the doctors given you a timetable for when you can start surfing or playing basketball again?"

Ashley's face brightened at the question.

"If I stick to my physical therapy, they say I could be back on my board by spring. I won't be doing aerials for a while. But I just want to get back out there, you know? Basketball's a little rougher. This will be a lost season. And the doctors don't want me doing any impact sports until next fall anyway. So we'll just have to see on that one."

"Well, I'd love to come to one of your games," Keri said. "Or even before that, maybe you could give me a surfing lesson or two. I've always wanted to learn."

Ashley giggled. Apparently the thought of Keri Locke on a surfboard was inherently funny. Just then, the maid poked her head in.

"Miss Ashley, your physical therapist is here for your afternoon session," she said.

"Thanks, Maricela," Ashley said, then turned to Keri. "My work is never done. I have morning, afternoon, and evening sessions. At least the evening guy is cute."

"Ashley Penn, please steer clear of guys for a little while, especially the cute ones," Keri said, surprised at how mom-ish she sounded.

Ashley laughed out loud. The sound gave Keri a hit of pure joy. After everything the girl had been through, the fact that she retained her sense of humor was something of a miracle.

Ashley must have been thinking the same thing because the laugh quickly gave way to tears. Keri slid over and wrapped her arms around the teenager, who squeezed her back tight.

"I still have nightmares about him," Ashley whispered in her ear between sniffles. "I picture myself strapped into that machine, my arms and legs being pulled in different directions, him standing over me, getting pleasure from my agony."

"I know," Keri whispered back, holding the shaking teen close. "I have them too. But I promise, they'll fade over time."

"Are you sure?" Ashley asked quietly. Keri pulled back so the girl could look into her eyes.

"I am. I've seen a lot of terrible things, Ashley. And almost all of them fade with time. This will too. Just don't shut down. Keep talking to your doctors, your therapists, your mom, to me. And remember. Alan Pachanga is in a hole in the ground. Next spring you'll be doing air spirals in the ocean."

"Aerials," Ashley said, breaking into a little grin.

"Yeah, those. Listen, I'm going to go. You've got your physical therapy and I have to make Los Angeles safe for juvenile delinquents like you. But I'd like to visit again if that's okay. Maybe next week?"

"I'd really like that," Ashley said.

They hugged one last time. Then Keri headed out. As she left the room she exchanged glances with the security guard near the door. He nodded politely and Keri thought she might have seen a tear trickling down his cheek. She hoped it wasn't her imagination.

As she headed back to the car, she couldn't help but be impressed with the kid's resilience. In the last three weeks, she'd been abducted and tortured, broken multiple bones in her body, discovered her uncle was a murderous sociopath, and learned her parents were getting divorced. And still, she saw Keri off with an authentic smile on her face.

As she got in the car, Keri wondered if she might be better off replacing some of her Glenlivet time with visits to other kids she'd helped. It was definitely a healthier way to get a rush.

Of course, not every kid bounced back like Ashley had. And not every vengeful control freak acted out by pushing for foreclosures and zoning violations. Some of them took their revenge in more personal, intimate ways.

A thought began to dart in and out of Keri's mind, just out of reach, like a wisp of smoke she couldn't quite grab hold of. Keri closed her eyes and breathed deeply, trying to force all the extraneous junk out and focus on the idea that was teasing her, so close to showing itself.

Control is everything. Order must be maintained. Chaos must be punished. Vengeance must be had. Personal. Intimate. Retribution.

Without warning, an image popped into her head, seemingly out of nowhere. It was of the receptionist in Dr. Burlingame's office earlier. She'd looked almost frightened when she'd realized she hadn't seen the note about Keri's appointment in the computer. And then there was the nurse, so hesitant to interrupt their conversation, so quick to leave once she'd been rebuked.

What made them both so edgy? Lots of doctors are short with their staff. There is that whole God Complex thing. But this somehow seemed like something more.

Keri remembered how Mags had said Jeremy wasn't interested in kids. And that made sense. Children are messy, not just physically but emotionally. They disrupt an ordered life.

But to reject your wife's desire to have a child under any circumstances—no adoption, no surrogate—just because it would be a hassle? That's taking the need for a tidy life to another level.

Still, none of these things were crimes. They weren't evidence of anything more than him being an ultra-anal, type-A asshole.

Besides, Jeremy Burlingame wanted to pursue his wife's case even as the police were planning to close it. He offered to take a polygraph. He seemed truly devastated at the news that Kendra had cheated. And he had an alibi.

Or did he? Keri remembered that his alibi had been verified by Detective Frank Brody, the laziest, most slovenly cop she'd ever met and one who was just months from retirement. It wasn't a stretch to think he might not have pursued every lead vigorously.

Keri picked up her phone and searched for the number she needed. After she found it, she punched in the digits and waited. While the phone rang, it occurred to her that she was about to violate Hillman's specific directive not to pursue the case.

A male voice picked up and said, "Hello."

It wasn't too late. She could still hang up. She could still just go home and sleep.

"Hello?" the voice said again.

Last chance, Keri. Just hang up.

She didn't hang up.

CHAPTER TWENTY NINE

Keri gulped hard, ignored the part of her that said she was making a career-ending mistake, and spoke.

"Hello, this is Detective Keri Locke of the LAPD. To whom am I speaking?"

"This is Dr. Vijay Patel of San Diego Plastic Surgery Associates. What can I do for you, Detective?"

"I'm calling about a colleague of yours, Dr. Jeremy Burlingame."

"Yes, another detective from your department was here the other day asking questions about Dr. Burlingame as well."

"Right, I'm just following up. My understanding is that he was in surgery the whole time he was down there. Is that correct?"

"Yes. That was my recollection and I conferred with several other doctors and nurses to be sure. He arrived at the hospital around nine thirty in the morning. We began the procedure just after ten a.m. It ran until around two thirty p.m. He was there the whole time, except for one very brief break."

"I guess everyone needs a bathroom break," Keri joked.

"I suppose that's possible, Detective," Dr. Patel answered without a trace of humor, "although it would have been an extremely brief one."

"What do you mean?" Keri asked politely, although she felt her breathing quicken.

"I suppose I'm just being temperamental. You see, the closest restroom is a good three-minute walk from the surgical suite. It's something we've repeatedly complained about to the administration."

"I'm not sure I take your point, Doctor," Keri said, confused.

"It's just that he was gone less than five minutes. Not really enough time to do much of anything, if you get my meaning."

Keri let that sink in.

What other reason could Burlingame have for stepping out in the middle of an involved procedure?

"I see," she said. "Is it possible he stepped out to take a call or check a voicemail or text?"

"It would be unusual to have a phone in the operating room at all," Dr. Patel said. "Generally it's not allowed. They're not sterile and sudden ringing or buzzing can be a big deal when you have a scalpel in your hand."

"Did you hear any buzzing?" Keri asked hopefully.

"No, I didn't. And to be honest, Detective Locke, I probably wouldn't have said anything even if I had. Dr. Burlingame made a special trip down to assist us. He did it completely pro bono. No one was going to make a fuss over any of his peculiarities. If he needed to take a half dozen breaks during the procedure, we would have been happy to accommodate him."

Keri could sense the doctor getting impatient and decided to wrap things up.

"Of course. How nice of him to go all the way down to San Diego and spend so many fully accounted-for hours with your team. One more thing, when did he step out?"

"It was pretty early on. Maybe ten thirty a.m. give or take."

"And you said he was gone less than five minutes?"

"Yes, and that includes having to re-gown and scrub back in."

"Thanks, Dr. Patel. You've been very gracious. We'll try not to bother you again."

Keri hung up and sat quietly in the car for a moment.

Why am I still obsessing over Jeremy Burlingame? Is it because things went sideways with the Collector and I have to have someone else to pick on? The man has been more supportive of my investigation than my own boss. And yet I keep coming at him. This is turning into a witch hunt.

After a minute, she started the car, pulled into traffic, and dialed Kevin Edgerton's number.

If this doesn't pan out, let it go.

"Edgerton here."

"Kevin, I need a favor."

"Keri, what are you doing calling in? The lieutenant said not to call you about the case."

"I'm calling you, so you're not in trouble. Why would you call me? Do you have new info or something?"

"No," Edgerton said unconvincingly.

"You're a terrible liar. Just tell me what it is."

"No way. What if Hillman comes back and hears me? He'll kill me."

"So he's not there—great. You have no excuse now."

"I can't."

"Kevin, tell me what you have or I'm coming into the station right now. And when Hillman sees me, I'll rat you out."

"Okay, jeez. It's just the fingerprints. We've got IDs on every recognizable print."

"And...?"

"Kendra Burlingame isn't among them. Although Palm Springs PD says there were still nine partial prints they just couldn't ID."

"So we still don't know definitively if Kendra was ever in that bus station or if the woman we saw was her," Keri said.

"Hillman thinks she was one of those nine partials. He's ready to close the case. In fact, I think he's going to sign the paperwork when he gets back."

"Where is he now?" she asked.

"He went to get a bite—left a few minutes ago."

"Good," Keri said, "then you have to do that favor I asked of you."

"What is it?"

"I know Suarez already did this. But I want you to check Jeremy Burlingame's cell phone records again, specifically for any incoming or outgoing calls on Monday morning between ten and eleven a.m."

"Come on, Keri. I could hear Hillman screaming at you earlier about bothering that guy."

"No one's bothering him," Keri insisted. "We're just looking up some phone numbers. It's harmless. And while you're at it, I need you to do one more thing."

"You're killing me. I literally feel the life force leaving my body."

"Don't be a wuss, Kevin. I need you to go back through the train station footage," she said, ignoring him. "You're looking to see if the headscarf woman ever makes a phone call. I don't remember one and I think I would have noticed it. But just in case."

"Anything else?" he asked sarcastically.

"Yes, please. Pull up the photos of the folks who were identified from the fingerprints."

"Why?"

"Because I'm going to want to look at them when I get to the office in five minutes."

She hung up before he could respond.

*

No one said anything to Keri as she walked across the bullpen to Edgerton's desk, but she could see a bunch of people looking at her in shock out of the corner of their eyes. She ignored them all.

"Give me good news," she said as she pulled up a chair and sat down next to Edgerton, who was staring at his computer monitor.

"I don't know if it's good, but I have news," he said, pointing at a phone number on the screen. "There's no call to or from Dr. Burlingame's cell phone during the window you gave me."

Keri's heart sank. She had been sure he'd made or received a call or text. What other reason would he have for stepping out of surgery for such a brief period?

Maybe he had a cramp. Maybe he had to fart. Maybe he just needed a private moment to regroup. You do that all the time.

"Could he have used a burner phone?" she asked, aware that she sounded desperate now.

"Sure. But I'd have no record of that," Edgerton answered.

"Okay, were you able to check the bus station footage to see if our mystery woman was on the phone in the time window around ten thirty a.m.?"

"I was not."

"Why not?" she demanded, her voice rising.

"Why don't I just show you?" he said, pulling up the video, which was cued to 10:22 a.m.

He hit play and Keri watched as the woman walked down a hall and rounded the corner. Another camera picked her up as she turned right and walked through a door marked "Women." Edgerton hit pause. The time on the screen read 10:23 a.m.

"She was in the bathroom?" Keri asked.

"She was in the bathroom," Edgerton confirmed, smiling. "And look what time she leaves."

He fast-forwarded until the woman left the bathroom, notably not wearing her gloves. The time said 10:31 a.m.

"So she could have made a call during that time?" Keri said.

"It's not definitive. It's not proof of anything. But yes, she could have. Or she could have just had digestive problems."

"And there's no way to track if a call made from that bathroom on a burner phone went to a burner phone at the hospital in San Diego?"

"That's a real stretch, Keri. First of all, there's no evidence that anyone made any calls on any phone at any time. It's all just your speculation."

"Wow—that's a little harsh," Keri said, though she knew he was right.

"I'm just stating the facts, Keri. Even if that was our working theory, it would require weeks to untangle call records. Even then, we couldn't identify who made any of those calls. And need I remind you, Hillman's closing this case completely when he gets back."

Keri slumped in the chair. She was out of ideas. In addition to having no reason to suspect Burlingame, it seemed there was no way to prove anything even if she did.

People do sometimes just run away. Not everyone is a victim.

"But…" Edgerton said quietly, hesitantly, almost in a whisper.

Keri's head popped up immediately. There was something in Edgerton's voice. It reminded her of Evie's voice when she found an unexpected cookie at the bottom of the jar. It was the sound of someone who'd discovered buried treasure.

CHAPTER THIRTY

Keri's whole body tingled. All the aching seemed to have subsided. She looked at Edgerton excitedly and could tell immediately that there was more.

"What is it?" she asked.

He sighed heavily before pulling up a series of DMV photos.

"What are these?"

But then she realized what she was looking at. These were all the people whose fingerprints had been identified on the snow globes in the bus station gift shop. There were sixty-seven photos in all.

"Can you screen out all the men and any women not between thirty and fifty years old?"

The speed with which he completed the task suggested to Keri that this wasn't the first time he'd tried this filter.

After he was done, the monitor displayed eight women. Five of them were clearly not a match. Four were seriously overweight. One's license listed her as five foot two.

Of the three remaining women, none fit perfectly. One was blonde and at forty-six, was at the outer range of the age limit. Another was probably too short at five foot seven and at thirty, she just looked too young. The final woman was brunette and about the right height. But her jaw line was so square and pronounced that even without ever getting a clear look at the woman in the bus station footage, it was clear that they weren't the same person.

"I'm sorry, Keri. I checked all of them earlier. I didn't want to tell you because I knew you were hoping. But none of them looks to be a match, not even close. This just reinforced the lieutenant's confidence that it was Burlingame herself in the video. That's why he was so comfortable closing the case."

Keri stared at the screen, going over each of the women more closely. She felt that itch again, the sense that there was something right in front of her if she could just look at it from the proper perspective.

Her mind drifted to her own recent adventure, trying to avoid detection as she navigated her way through a building littered with security cameras.

I managed to get away with it—at least so far. It is possible.

"Show me the blonde again," she said suddenly. Edgerton pulled up her license full screen. It read:

JENNIFER HORNER, 46 YRS OLD, 5 FOOT 9, 125 LBS., SHERMAN OAKS, CA

Horner had renewed her license just two years ago so it wasn't too dated. Her short pixie-style haircut flattered her, making her look younger than her age, as did her immaculate makeup. It was one of the best DMV photos Keri could recall ever seeing.

"What does Jennifer do for a living, Kevin?" Keri asked as she looked into the woman's eyes.

"She's a makeup artist. It looks like she mostly works on crappy reality shows. The license says Sherman Oaks but she lives in Silverlake now. She's single. Has a sister who also lives in town. No obvious connections to the Burlingames as far as I can tell."

"Are you able to make alterations to her DMV image, Photoshop it a bit?"

"I guess but it'll be pretty rough."

"That's okay. Give her long dark hair."

Edgerton's fingers zipped around the keyboard and mouse. It took less than thirty seconds for Jennifer to become a brunette.

"Now give her sunglasses and a headscarf like the other woman."

That process took only two minutes. Without being asked, Edgerton pulled up a screen grab of the woman in bus station footage and placed it side by side with Horner's retouched DMV photo.

Keri stifled a gasp, not wanting to influence her colleague.

"What do you think?" she asked.

"I think maybe we shouldn't close this case. They could be twins."

Keri nodded, trying to keep cool and not let the sudden rush of euphoria she felt overwhelm her. The train station footage was grainy but there was no doubt that these two women looked shockingly similar.

Finally, a break!

"You willing to say that to Hillman?" Keri asked. Seeing him hesitate, she continued before he could reply. "How about before we take that step, you call Ms. Horner? Hillman says I can't do it...or anything. Let's find out where she is now. If she picks up the call and agrees to come in for an interview this afternoon, we know we have the wrong gal."

"I'm still not sure any of this is enough to go after Burlingame."

"It's not. Technically, these things are completely unrelated. Just like it may only be bad luck that the bus station woman never, not once, looks up so we can get a quality, head-on shot of her."

"Awfully suspicious though," Edgerton said.

"Yep," Keri agreed. "Just like it's suspicious that she never takes off her sunglasses or headscarf the whole morning, even though she's indoors. And maybe it's only a coincidence that the camera angles that would best help us ID this woman—the ones at the entrance to the bus station and on the bus itself—were both down that morning. None of it is enough to take to a prosecutor. There's no evidence that any crime has taken place."

"So what do we do now?" Edgerton asked.

Keri sat quietly beside him pondering the same question. An idea started to form in her head but before she could get it out, her phone rang. It was from her department-assigned psychiatrist, Dr. Beverly Blanc. Keri was required to check in with her periodically.

"I've got to take this," she told Edgerton as she got up to leave. "But here's what you should do. Try to contact Jennifer Horner. If you can't, reach out to her sister and her employer. If they can't account for her whereabouts, let Interpol know to be on the lookout for her, specifically in Barcelona."

"And I assume you're going home to take a nap?" he said sarcastically.

"That's right, Kevin. I'm certainly not going to look for evidence that a crime has taken place. At least as far as Hillman knows."

CHAPTER THIRTY ONE

Keri tried to keep her cool but it wasn't easy. As she sat in her car in the police station parking lot and listened to her psychiatrist, she was getting more anxious, not less.

Isn't therapy supposed to reduce my stress, not increase it?

"Keri," Dr Beverly Blanc said in her perpetually cool but concerned tone, "Lieutenant Hillman really sounded like he was on the verge of dismissing you. I've never heard him so angry."

Keri hated that she was required to see a mental health professional but all things considered, she could do worse than Beverly Blanc. The woman was no-nonsense. She genuinely seemed to care about Keri's well-being. And she didn't pester her with annoying calls all the time. But her description of Hillman set Keri on edge.

"No offense, Doc. But I hear him that angry multiple times a day. It's not that big a deal."

"Have you ever considered why you always seem to be there when he blows his stack? Do you think there might be some connection there?"

Keri considered it. As usual, Dr. Blanc might have a point.

"What are you asking me to do?" she asked as she started her car and pulled out of the lot.

"Listen, you've told me about this Burlingame case and I can tell you're frustrated that you're not being allowed to pursue it. I can also sense that there's something else going on that you're not telling me about. I suspect it has to do with Evie but I'm not going to take that up for now."

"I appreciate that."

"What I am doing is asking you to follow your boss's orders," Dr. Blanc said. "Go home. Rest. Or go to a support group meeting. It's five thirty-five right now. There are several six p.m. meetings I can direct you to. Or come in and see me. I'm through with appointments for the day."

"Thanks, Doc. That's very generous of you. But I'm good."

"Are you, Keri? You say that but you're still so closed off. When are you going to come out of your cocoon?"

"With you on my side, I'll be a beautiful butterfly in no time."

"I feel like you're not taking me seriously."

"I am but I have to go. You know, to nap."

"Keri…" Dr. Blanc started to say.

"Thanks, Doc. Got to go."

Keri hung up and pulled over on the side of the road. Something Dr. Blanc had said about cocoons had triggered a vague memory for her.

It was a couple of years ago. She had been on the houseboat late one night, channel surfing and scarfing down pizza, when she'd stumbled across a reality show about women unhappy with their appearance. They all agreed to undergo a weight loss and exercise program and to have plastic surgery. The show was called *Butterfly*.

Keri realized that was what the word in the corner of those photos in Burlingame's office referred to. Those women were contestants on the show and he must have been one of the plastic surgeons.

She did a search on her phone to see what reality shows Jennifer Horner had worked on as a makeup artist. Sure enough, there it was. She was credited as "head makeup artist" on the show's one season before it was cancelled due to poor ratings.

There was no proof yet that she and Burlingame had ever interacted. That would require interviews with the crew of the show. But finding and interviewing those people, all now working on other series, would require time and manpower, neither of which she currently had.

If the woman at that bus station and on the flight to Barcelona was Jennifer Horner, then Kendra Burlingame was missing. And someone wanted to keep that from the world. Keri didn't have enough to arrest Jeremy Burlingame or even to get a search warrant. She didn't have the support of her superior or anything other than circumstantial evidence and her gut instinct.

But that was enough for her. So she turned her car around and headed north, in the direction of Beverly Hills. She was going to the Burlingame mansion.

CHAPTER THIRTY TWO

Keri was in serious discomfort. She had been kneeling in the bushes near the outer gate of the Burlingame compound for nearly fifteen minutes. Her thighs were burning and her ribs were starting to throb under the strain of being in a crouch for so long. It didn't help that she was wearing her bulletproof vest, which weighed her down even more.

She could see Lupe, the maid, going back and forth to her car in the roundabout and suspected she was preparing to leave for the night.

But she was taking her sweet time and Keri was running out of it. She looked at her watch. It was 6:29 p.m. Burlingame had told her he had appointments today until seven. That didn't give her a ton of time to search the house for evidence and get out undetected before he got home.

At 6:30 p.m. exactly Lupe walked out for what appeared to be the last time and got in her car. Apparently she was a real stickler for not leaving early, even when she was the only one there. As she approached the gate, she clicked a remote to open it. She eased out onto the driveway connected to the residential street.

Keri forced herself to stay low and still, even though she desperately wanted to dash through the gate. She checked her waistband for about the fifth time. Everything was still there—her gun, her handcuffs, her Taser.

Halfway down the driveway, Lupe saw the large rock Keri had placed there earlier. She put her car in park and got out to move it. Only when Keri was sure the maid was focused on that task and couldn't just glance back in the rearview mirror did she rush from her hiding spot, dart through the gate just before it slammed shut, and hide behind a large stone pillar.

She peeked out in time to see Lupe toss the rock into the grass. The maid gave one last look back at the mansion, returned to her car, and drove off. Keri was alone.

She moved quickly. The sun was already starting to set and within the next half hour she'd be in relative darkness. If Kendra Burlingame was being kept hidden somewhere on the compound, she only had a short time to find her.

She started outside, checking a gardening shed and then the pool house. There was nothing out of the ordinary in either. She banged on the walls of each and stamped on the floors, feeling for hollow spots that might suggest hidden rooms. Nothing.

Then she moved to the house itself. She'd checked on the drive up to the mansion to see if the Burlingames used a security system. Apparently they had one but only used it when they were traveling. Still a little worried, she delicately jimmied the lock to the kitchen door, opened it, and waited for any beeping or siren. She heard nothing.

After a minute, she felt confident enough to enter. She used the floor plans she'd downloaded earlier to make her way straight to Dr. Burlingame's study. She didn't bother going through his papers. If he was behind this, it was highly unlikely that he'd leave proof of it in easily discovered documents in his office.

Instead, she looked around for anything that seemed out of the ordinary: Indentations on the hardwood floor that might suggest furniture had recently been moved. Unusual drafts of air that might indicate a hidden room. She again knocked on the walls, but they were all solid.

Next she moved upstairs to the bedroom to get a better look around than the last time she was there.

Arguments often started in the bedroom and could easily escalate. If there was some kind of physical altercation, this might be the best place to find evidence of it.

But nothing seemed odd. No picture frames were out of place, no wall paintings were askew, no bloodstains were hidden under area rugs. Of course, Lupe would have corrected the first two, so drawing any conclusions was probably pointless.

Keri moved into the bathroom and looked around. Nothing jumped out at her. There was a long counter with dual sinks. One side was immaculate, with everything—razor, toothbrush, comb, hand towel—it its proper place. The other looked like a tornado had ripped through it.

Keri moved closer to the section that Kendra obviously used and studied it. Strewn out next to the sink were a hair dryer, a plastic tub full to the brim with makeup, two hairbrushes, and a long lonely strand of floss. The only things obviously missing were a toothbrush, toothpaste, and any medication.

That made sense if one bought the theory that Kendra had bailed and only taken the essentials. It also made sense if one suspected that the sink was carefully set up to create that impression.

Keri turned off the light and pulled her trusty flashlight out of her pocket. In one mode it was a traditional flashlight. But push a button and it became a black light, which used UV rays to detect material invisible to the naked eye.

She shined it carefully over the floor, searching for any hint that blood might have been spilled in the room. Finding nothing, she moved over to the tub and shower. Still nothing.

Keri looked at her watch. It was 7:04 p.m. Burlingame would be done with his final appointment of the day by now. If he headed back immediately, he could be back at the house in thirty to forty-five minutes. She had to be long gone by then. Running out of time, she tried to focus.

Where else might a meticulous, controlling type do his dirty work?

And then it popped into her head, so obvious that she felt like kicking herself. Keri rushed down the stairs, ignoring her still-sore ribs and shoulder, and made her way to the garage. She opened the door and turned on the light. It was empty, of course. Kendra's car was with the Palm Springs police and Jeremy was currently driving his here.

But even so, it looked like it was rarely used for the cars. The floor was spotless and the tools along the far wall were perfectly organized.

Excited, Keri turned off the overhead light and tried her black light again. But there wasn't a hint of blood anywhere on the floor. Keri turned the main light back on and sat on the garage step, trying not to let her frustration overwhelm her investigative sense.

Was it possible that she was wrong about all of this? That it was all just a big coincidence and Kendra had really run off to Spain? While it didn't seem likely, it wasn't inconceivable that both Kendra and Jennifer Horner had been at the Palm Springs bus station in the last few days.

There was even the chance that Jennifer had developed some sort of fixation on the Burlingames and pulled some kind *Talented Mr. Ripley*–style identity theft scheme. Keri doubted it but if she was honest, she'd never really even thought to chase that lead.

For that matter, she'd never seriously pursued the possibility that Lupe the maid was somehow involved; or Becky, the cokehead friend; or even Mags. She'd left a lot of stones unturned.

Regardless of what had happened, she had to admit that she hadn't found a single definitive shred of evidence that Jeremy Burlingame had done anything wrong.

She stood up and wandered over to the wall of tools, absently perusing them as she turned over the possibilities in her head. Most of them, despite being well organized, were caked in dirt. Apparently cleaning gardening tools wasn't in Lupe's job description. Considering how worn and grimy many of them were,

Keri suspected that the less fastidious Kendra had the family's green thumb.

Finally, she came to the shovel at the far end of the wall. Surprisingly, it looked to be in pretty good shape. In fact, it was so clean that it appeared like it had never been used. Keri turned it over and saw that it still had the barcode and Home Depot stickers on the back.

Every other tool in this garage is dirty. But this shovel has never been used. It looks like it was just bought to replace an old one. But why would the old one need to be replaced? Unless it was broken. Or there was something incriminating about it.

Suddenly Keri realized she'd been searching in the wrong place.

CHAPTER THIRTY THREE

She grabbed the shovel and ran outside, trying to control the adrenaline shooting through her system. It was almost completely dark now and she struggled to find her way to the spot she was looking for.

Eventually she got sight of the lighted pool in the distance and used that to guide her to her destination. When she got there she knew she had the right place.

She stared down into deep pit beside the pool that had been excavated to make room for the hot tub that was being built. The pit was a good five feet deep now. But there was no reason the Bobcat couldn't have created a hole much deeper, where a body could be buried and covered over.

But using an industrial excavator to pour the dirt back over the hole would have been risky. If something went wrong, it could accidentally dig back into the hole, risking cutting into the body below.

Better to use a shovel to cover it up and just use the Bobcat to pat the earth down firmly afterward. But who knows what human DNA might accidentally get on that shovel when it was burying the body? The safe move was to dispose of it and just get a new one.

Keri was just about to jump into the hole and start digging when her phone buzzed. It was Edgerton. She picked up,

"What is it, Kevin? I'm a little busy here."

"You said to call when I had some information. So I'm calling."

"Sorry. Go ahead."

"We just got a hit on Jennifer Horner," he said.

"Great. Where is she?"

"She's dead."

"What?" Keri asked, unsure if she'd heard him right.

"She was found in a Barcelona hotel a few hours ago. The full autopsy results won't be ready for weeks but the pathologist told me it looks like she's been poisoned."

"How is that possible?"

"They found massive amounts of potassium in her system."

"Potassium? Like in bananas?"

"Yes, but this was over five hundred times what you'd find in a banana. In doses that high, it causes kidney and heart failure. But it was slow-acting, so it took about three days to have its full effect. That explains why she was able to travel for a while. And Keri, only a medical professional could access it in amounts that large."

"You know what this means, right, Kevin?"

"It means Burlingame was eliminating the one person who could rat him out."

"Exactly. And I found a connection between the two of them. They both worked—"

Keri head a twig snap behind her and started to turn around. But before she could, she felt a massive explosion of pain in the back of her head and then everything went black.

*

She heard sounds before she could see anything.

Keri wasn't sure how long she'd been unconscious. But she knew it hadn't been a fainting spell. Someone had whacked her in the head.

As she lay there trying to get her bearings and ignore the screaming agony in her skull, Keri could tell somebody was moving around nearby. There was also a loud humming sound, metallic in nature.

Then she felt a sudden shock of weight land on her. It took everything she had not to grunt audibly. The stab of pain that shot through her body immediately cleared her ringing head.

She could smell something familiar in the air and kind of taste it too. After a moment, she realized what it was—dirt. She was being covered in dirt.

And then she recognized what the metallic humming was—the Bobcat. Someone had turned it on and was using it to dump the extra dirt on top of her.

She squinted her eyes open just a bit. It took a second to understand what she was seeing. She was in the hot tub hole, lying on her back. Most of her body was covered in dirt. She couldn't see her legs but she could tell they'd been somehow bound at the ankles. Her hands were free but weighed down by dozens of pounds of dirt.

No one was visible but she heard the Bobcat getting closer. The lights of the machine grew brighter. All of a sudden it was right above her, at the edge of the hole. The bucket dumped a huge mound of earth on top of her and she felt it starting to crush her chest. She couldn't tell whether the pain she felt was her ribs being destroyed anew or a brand new kind of torture.

As she tried to inhale, some of the dirt went down her throat and she coughed involuntarily. The Bobcat engine suddenly eased down and she heard footsteps.

"Look who's awake," she heard a familiar voice say.

The figure stepped in front of the excavator's headlights and she saw him: Jeremy Burlingame. He appeared calm and impassive, as if burying an LAPD detective alive was just a regular evening's activity.

He was dressed in his dress shirt and slacks from this afternoon, although he'd removed the jacket and tie. There was a thin line of sweat on his brow and tiny stains under his armpits. But otherwise, he looked unruffled.

"I'm so sorry it had to come to this, Detective Locke. It's not how I wanted this to go at all. It's just that I heard you talking on the phone. I heard the word 'potassium' and realized you had to know about Jennifer. And here I thought I had planned that out so well. But I guess it's true what they say—there really is no such thing as the perfect crime. That's really disappointing, considering all my hard work. I just have to know, how did you find out about her?"

Keri coughed some more, then spit out the remaining dirt in her mouth before whispering to him.

"Hard…to …speak with…this on…chest."

"I would imagine so. Just shimmy a little and it should fall to the sides a bit. That should help."

While he waited, she rocked her shoulders a bit and some of the dirt did slide off enough for her to breathe a little easier. As the weight subsided, she shoved her hands through the dirt until they were at her waistband. She felt around but couldn't find what she was searching for.

"Looking for this?" Burlingame asked as he held up her belt with her gun, cuffs, and Taser attached. "Or maybe you were after your phone? Here it is."

With that he kicked the smashed wreckage of her phone into the pit with her. She saw he was holding something between his thumb and forefinger. He continued.

"Sorry. I had to remove the locater. Can't have your police buddies finding you too soon, you know. I mean, they're going to find you eventually. But it'll be too late to do you much good—or to do me much harm."

"No alibi…for …this," she muttered hoarsely.

"That's true. It's a little frustrating, I have to admit. I put so much energy into my alibi for Kendra's disappearance and to not have anything for you, it's quite embarrassing. Luckily, I have a contingency plan."

"What's…that?" Keri asked.

163

Just keep him talking. He seems to like that. He hasn't had anyone to share his master plan with. He wants to gloat. He wants to be admired and respected. The longer he discusses his brilliance, the more time I have to figure out a way out of this hellhole.

"I really shouldn't tell you. But since you'll be dead soon, I feel like you deserve to know. Let's just say that I've been planning for a quick escape ever since I hatched this little plan well over a year ago.

"There's a pilot on call with a plane at the Santa Monica airport. He'll happily take me to a country I'd rather not name. But it doesn't have an extradition treaty with the US. Nor do any of the four other countries I have set up as backups should things get complicated. I had hoped to stay here and live out my years as the wronged, sainted husband who still held a torch for his missing wife. But spending my life sipping rum drinks on the beach is an okay backup plan."

"But... why?" Keri asked, half stalling, half genuinely wanting an answer. "She loved you."

Suddenly, the unruffled expression on his face disappeared, replaced by something she'd never seen before—pure, twisted fury.

Without speaking, he turned and walk out of her sight. She heard the Bobcat start up again and saw the shadow of the bucket drop down to collect a new pile of dirt. In the brief unwatched moment she had, Keri felt around until she reached her back pocket. To her relief, her small flashlight was still there. She pulled it out and held it tight against her chest, just as a new round of dirt slammed down on her, covering her waist, chest, and face.

She had been holding her breath so it took a few seconds to realize there was so much earth covering her face that she couldn't breathe.

Keri was suffocating.

CHAPTER THIRTY FOUR

She tried not to panic. With her right hand clutching the flashlight, Keri had no choice but to force her left arm up, ignoring the howling anguish in her shoulder, as she reached up to rip and tear the heavy mound of dirt away from her face.

As she gasped and coughed, Burlingame reappeared. The enraged glare was gone now. He looked like his old self.

"Sorry, Detective. But I couldn't let that kind of comment stand. The notion that such an adulteress loved me is offensive. And to think, if I hadn't been going through her jewelry box to find her favorite necklace so I could buy her a matching bracelet, I never would have found that hidden compartment. And I never would have seen the love letter from Alex Crane. And I never would have known that I was living with a lying, cheating bitch."

His face twisted up again at that last line but he managed to regain control. Keri needed him to keep talking, even if it risked angering him.

"It was…five years ago. It was in… past. She didn't tell you …because she didn't…want…hurt you." It was hard to get full breaths. Keri worried that another mound of earth might be too much for her to handle.

"She shamed herself," Burlingame said. "And she shamed me. God knows how many of her friends knew that she'd been sneaking off, and with some new age, wannabe lothario from her yoga class? I have no doubt that whenever her friends saw me, they thought 'there goes the pathetic cuckold.' I was oblivious for years, a target of derision and laughter. And not because of anything I did. But because of her!"

"So… solution was…to…kill her? Couldn't just…divorce?"

"No. She had to pay a steeper price than that. I wasn't going to pay alimony to that harlot. She had to know I had uncovered her crime. She had to face the consequences fully. That's why it took so long, Detective. Finding the right substitute woman to make Kendra's 'escape' from town; setting up a fake passport and credit cards for her; teaching Jennifer all the details of her assignment and how to avoid detection and identification along the way; disabling the proper cameras at the bus station and on the bus; organizing my future accommodations in multiple non-extradition countries; and of course, the potassium. Detective, you can't imagine how difficult it was to accumulate enough for the job without drawing suspicion—very tricky."

His eyes were blazing with a crazed fervor. He was getting off on describing his exploits, pacing with manic energy. As he moved back and forth, his attention elsewhere, Keri shook off as much of the remaining dirt as she could without him noticing. Then she pulled her arms down and rested them at her sides.

When he turned back, she became still and asked another question she hoped would appeal to his ego.

"How did you...convince...Jennifer?"

"Oh, that was easy. I kept her in the dark about the true nature of things. But I knew from interacting with her on that atrocious reality show that she was a greedy, venal woman who was deep in debt and tired of the thankless grind of television production. When I told her that if she helped me, no questions asked, I'd give her half a million dollars, she jumped at the chance. Whatever suspicions she had, she very pointedly avoided asking me any questions. I think she was excited to live the expat life."

He laughed, apparently at the memory of her naiveté. After a moment, he went on.

"It evidently never occurred to her that I couldn't just wire a half million dollars to Europe without raising suspicions here. She was never even apprehensive that a man willing to engage in such mysterious, clearly nefarious behavior ought not to be trusted. No major loss, if you ask me."

As he spoke, Keri formulated the rough outline of a plan. It was crazy and desperate. But it was the only one she could think of under the circumstances. And for it to work, she'd need to bait him just enough, but not so much that he would return to burying her alive. She decided to give him one more ego boost before dropping the hammer.

"So your...alibi? It was real... because...you had already...killed Kendra?" she asked, intentionally playing up her very real shortness of breath.

Burlingame seemed delighted by her interest. It was hard to believe that this animated livewire was the same man who had been so composed and professional in their other encounters. No wonder he enjoyed plotting this elaborate crime. It was like a drug for him.

"Impressive, wasn't it. By making everyone think Kendra had run off or at the very least, was alive until mid-morning Monday, no one thought to check my alibi for any other time than that. But of course, if they'd checked my whereabouts on Sunday evening, they'd have learned that both Kendra and I were here. And by here, I mean literally right where you and I are now. I was dumping huge mounds of earth into this hole. And she was where you're lying, slowly choking to death, being buried alive. Maybe when I pound the dirt down on top of you, you'll see her with your own dead eyes."

Keri took in his words like a punch to the gut. Until now, some small part of her still held out hope that Kendra was still alive, being held in some hidden basement on the property. But hearing Burlingame describe her gruesome death so coldly, with such malevolent pleasure, that last little flicker of hope was extinguished.

She allowed herself to accept the truth: she had failed to save this woman, a person who, from all accounts, was kind and decent and deserved far better. But to Keri's surprise, the thought of Kendra's loss didn't evoke despair in her. Instead, she felt another, more powerful emotion rising in her chest: determination.

"Maybe," Keri finally said, deciding now was the moment to go for it, before he followed through on his threat. "Or maybe...you'll   screw   that...up...just   like...you...did with...Jennifer. I... outsmarted you...on...that...one."

By the end of her sentence, Keri made sure that her voice was little more than a hoarse whisper. She could see him leaning in to hear her better.

"Yes, that really is the last mystery," he acknowledged. "You know, if you tell me how you identified Jennifer, I might be inclined to shoot you in the head before I bury you. Wouldn't that be preferable? What do you say, Detective? That's a fair exchange—your secret for my mercy."

"Yes. But...can't...breathe," Keri said, barely audible now.

This is it. Either he goes for it and I have a chance. Or he doesn't and I die.

"Oh, fine then. You've piqued my interest. After all, a good physician always learns from his mistakes," he said as he began to gingerly ease his way down into the pit. "You know, this is your fault, Detective. After all, I chose you specifically to handle my case."

Now down in the pit, he knelt beside her and began to shove the largest chunks of dirt off her chest.

"Why...me?" Keri asked as she braced herself for what was to come.

"Because I knew that if I could convince even you, the famous finder of the lost, that Kendra had run off, that I would be free and clear. Other cops, like your colleague Detective Brody, didn't need much inducement to buy my story. But if I insisted on keeping the case open—offering to take polygraphs, demanding to hire my own investigators—and even you agreed to close it, then I was home free. But you were like a dog with a bone, Detective. You just wouldn't give up. I guess I underestimated you, didn't I?"

He continued to slide the dirt off her chest, prattling on, not even looking at her. She opened her mouth and spoke so softly that Burlingame had to lean very close to hear her.

"Yes…you…did."

CHAPTER THIRTY FIVE

At that moment, and before Burlingame knew what was happening, Keri swung her right arm upward, hard and fast.

Out of the corner of his eye, Burlingame noticed the movement and started to turn his head. But he was too slow to stop the flashlight Keri gripped tightly from smashing into his right temple.

He seemed more surprised than dazed. But before he could react, Keri smashed him again in the same place, again and again, multiple times in quick succession. She pummeled him so hard that the light started to crack. A few times she missed her target and the light smashed into his cheek, ripping it open. Shards of plastic jutted out from his skin and blood started to pour from the wound at his temple.

Burlingame, bewildered, reached out wildly to grab the flashlight. But Keri avoided his hand and, taking the now jagged base of the light, jabbed hard and fast at the left side of his neck.

Blood spurted from it. She jabbed again, with even more force than the first time. The chunk of black plastic stuck there as blood gushed out all around it. Burlingame reached up to grab at it, his eyes frenzied.

As he did, Keri gathered all the force she could muster and used her right arm to shove him to the left so that he fell over her and landed on his back. She rolled over so that she was lying on top of him. He didn't seem to notice, as he was clawing furiously at the base of the flashlight, still lodged in the left side of his neck.

Keri grabbed his shoulders to brace herself as she yanked her bent legs up to rest on his mid-section. Her ankles were still tied together so the maneuver was clumsy and she almost toppled over.

But she managed to right herself just as Burlingame yanked what was left of the flashlight from his neck. Wild with panic and rage in them, his eyes locked on her hers.

They moved at the same time. He brought the flashlight husk up hard, hoping to do the same thing to her that she'd done to him. As he did, Keri thrust her forearm out to block him. Her arm smashed into his wrist and the light slipped out of his blood-soaked hand and landed harmlessly several feet away.

Without pausing, Keri flung both hands around his neck, running thick with deep red blood. He began to punch at her, swinging wildly, sometimes making contact with her jaw or shoulder, other times missing completely.

Keri ignored it all. All her focus was on wringing every ounce of breath out of the man until he was still. After what felt like an eternity, the pounding from his fists grew weaker and finally stopped altogether. His arms dropped limp at his sides. And still she squeezed, pressing in on him until her hands were numb and her arms had no strength left at all.

Only then did she let go, allowing herself to collapse in the dirt beside him. She lay there for some time, her chest heaving between occasional fits of coughing. Eventually she rolled over to a sitting position and reached down to untie her bound ankles.

She pulled herself up to her knees, then used the wall of the pit for support as she slowly stood up. She slumped against the side of the pit, resting there as she waited for her strength to return.

The lights from the Bobcat still shined into the pit, illuminating Burlingame in its harsh gleam. She looked down at him—at his lifeless body, at his ruined face, at his eyes, now cloudy, devoid of all the mania that had consumed them only minutes earlier.

After a couple more moments of slow, steady breathing, she gathered herself for one more task. And then Detective Keri Locke pulled herself out of the pit and walked away. She didn't look back.

CHAPTER THIRTY SIX

Her head, which had required sixteen stitches to patch up, was pounding relentlessly. It was like someone had inserted a mini-jackhammer in her skull. But this time around, Keri only had to stay in the hospital overnight. She'd been diagnosed with a bad concussion and the doctors wanted to monitor her for twenty-four hours before releasing her.

Other than that, the damage was minimal. Her face and shoulders were sore and discolored from where Burlingame had punched her. But she hardly noticed that. Amazingly the buckets of dirt dropped on her had only bruised her ribs, not broken them. She probably had her bulletproof vest to thank for that.

Other than giving her statement, Keri chose not to think about what had happened at the Burlingame mansion for the time being. There would be time to pore over every detail later; to come to terms with the fact that she had literally choked the life out of another human being with her bare hands; that she hadn't been able to save Kendra. For now, she kept those memories at arm's length and focused on the positive.

It wasn't so bad, being in the hospital. Officer Jamie Castillo came by to check on her.

"I never got the chance to properly thank you for what you did at the Promenade," Keri told her.

"No worries. I appreciate you having enough confidence in me to take a chance."

"Truthfully, I mostly picked you because you were close by, very green, and I knew you looked up to me. I was counting on that outweighing your sense of departmental duty."

"I know that," Castillo said, "but I appreciate it anyway. And I'm sorry it didn't work out. Hopefully that won't stop you from calling on me in the future."

"I'll keep you in mind," Keri said in a snarky tone that was undermined by the broad smile on her face.

After Castillo left, Keri was able to hang out with Ray, who was scheduled to be released sometime over the weekend. They played checkers, ate Jell-O, and perused websites for furniture to add to her new apartment in Playa del Rey. Keri still hadn't seen it but she trusted Ray and he trusted the apartment owner, Rene. That was good enough for her.

"How did physical therapy go earlier?" she asked him.

"Not too bad. They tell me that if I behave and don't over-exert myself, I can return to desk duty in a week and get back in the field in a month."

"That's great!"

"Yeah, but I don't know how I'm going to keep busy for a week," he said. "I think I'll go stir crazy just sitting in my place."

"Not if you focus on interior decorating," Keri said, nodding at the catalogue they'd been perusing. "I'm getting a little windfall from the houseboat sale and, in addition to the furniture, the new place still needs some homey touches, like art and rugs and flatware and, well, pretty much everything. You can be my personal Martha Stewart."

"Keri, I'm a former professional boxer and a decorated LAPD detective. I'm not a feng shui expert."

"I'm sure you'll do great. And if you screw up, I'll just replace it. You'll never know the difference.

"You're probably right," Ray said. "Are you going to wrap up the Burlingame case report soon?"

"Yep, probably on Sunday. I can pick you up afterwards."

"You know, everyone would have had it a lot easier if everyone had just listened to me from the beginning. I solved the case without even knowing any details."

"Oh yeah, how's that?" she asked with a smirk on her face.

"It's like I predicted, the husband did it."

"Okay, Columbo. I don't know how we managed without you."

"Me either."

He sat quietly for a second and she could tell he was about to get serious.

"What?" she asked.

"You never told me if anything came of that e-mail you sent to the Collector. That makes me think it didn't go well."

Keri debated how much to tell him right now. Her head still ached and she didn't really feel like revisiting the details of that awful day at the moment.

"Short version—he set up a meet in Santa Monica. I went, but for complicated reasons, it fell through. I think there's a chance he may reach out again so I'm forcing myself not to contact him for fear of scaring him off. You can imagine it hasn't been easy."

"I can," he said as he tried to get up to move from the chair to his bed. Keri stood to help him.

"Take it slow," she whispered.

"I will," he said, then added delicately, "Maybe you can give me the long version when you feel up to it?"

"Absolutely. Maybe when I take you home on Sunday."

"Home?" he said, disgruntled. "We're not going straight home."

"Where are we going?" she asked.

"To get coffee. You told me that on the way home, we could stop for coffee and talk about stuff, remember?"

Keri suddenly felt a nervous pit in her stomach but made sure not to let it show.

"I remember," she said, as she helped him to his feet.

"Good," he replied, wrapping his huge arm around her shoulder for support. "Because I always say, stuff is one of my favorite topics."

*

She got permission to be discharged on Friday evening and had just changed out of the hospital gown and back into her own clothes when she got a surprise visitor in her room: Jackson Cave.

He walked in unannounced as she was putting on her socks.

"Hello, Detective," he said as if his being there was the most natural thing in the world. "I was just visiting a client on the second floor and heard you were here. I had to stop by and offer my best wishes. But I do have to say, you seem to spend an inordinate amount of time in hospitals."

After the initial shock of seeing him there at all, Keri studied Cave hard, trying to determine if he knew about her late-night visit to his office earlier in the week. Neither his comments nor his body language betrayed anything. She forced herself to be equally inscrutable.

"I do use more of my healthcare dollars than the average person. But it's well worth it, in my opinion. You could ask Payton Penn about that. Or Alan Pachanga. Okay, maybe not him."

"No, Mr. Pachanga is certainly not available to comment. But I'm sure he's here with us in spirit. I feel like he's the kind of man who had much more to offer before he was taken from us."

"More to offer—like what?" Keri asked, wondering if this was just the sick admiration of one warped mind for another or a veiled reference to Pachanga's laptop, which had set her on the path that ultimately allowed her to crack Cave's code.

"That's the point. I guess we'll never know, will we? It's not like he can speak out from the grave and share his secrets, now is it?"

"I suppose not," Keri said, refusing to bite. "Was there anything else you wanted, Mr. Cave?"

"No. I just wanted to make sure you were well. And now that I see you are, I'll be on my way," he said, making his way to the door. "But I'm sure we'll be seeing each other again. You're a real comer, Detective Locke, and I've got my eye on you."

"Goodbye, Mr. Cave," Keri said, ignoring what she considered a threat.

He started to leave, pulling the door closed behind him, but then poked his head back in.

"If you don't mind my asking one last thing, Detective, I just wanted to know if you'd ever considered dyeing your hair."

"Why?"

"I think you'd look lovely as a brunette."

And then he was gone, leaving Keri alone in the room to try to get her shoes on and come to terms with the fact that he most certainly knew she had stolen his cipher. She tried to disregard the shiver that suddenly ran up her spine.

CHAPTER THIRTY SEVEN

Two days later, on Sunday morning, Keri woke up and felt genuinely good for the first time in almost three weeks.

Her ribs only really hurt when she coughed or laughed. Her shoulder was coming along more slowly but wasn't a constant source of pain anymore. Her head still ached dully but not so much that she couldn't function. And two consecutive nights of decent sleep had left her with more energy than she knew what to do with.

As she lay on the bunk in her houseboat for the last time, she reviewed her plans for what was turning out to be a busy day. The movers would be here at 9 a.m. to take what little stuff she had over to the apartment in Playa.

She was leaving most of the furniture here anyway and replacing it with items she'd ordered online while in the hospital. The marina management had offered to buy the boat "as is" from her and that money would pay for her new stuff and give her a decent nest egg for a few months. Besides, the entirety of her personal belongings could easily fit into the bed of a pickup truck, which was what the movers planned to use.

After she got squared away at the new place, she had to go into the station to finish up some paperwork on the Burlingame case. Lieutenant Hillman had let her hold off because of her hospital stay but now he was getting antsy to officially close the case and insisted she come in, even on a Sunday.

She needed to handle her report delicately, as she had broken into the mansion. If Burlingame had just shot her on sight, he might have had a case for self-defense. Luckily he had felt the need to share his brilliance with her before exacting some kind of poetic vengeance.

Now he was dead and she could say whatever she wanted in the police report. And what she intended to say was that she had gone to his house for an interview. When she turned her back, he knocked her out and threw her in the pit. Lying in her report wasn't exactly a source of pride. But she wasn't going to sweat it that much under the circumstances.

Kendra's body had indeed been found in the pit, about four feet below where her husband's ended up. The preliminary forensics indicated that Burlingame hadn't been lying when he'd said he buried her alive. The thought of the terror that woman must have felt in her last moments shook Keri to her core. It also wiped away what little guilt she was feeling about strangling a man who was probably only minutes away from dying anyway.

Burlingame had derisively called her "famous finder of the lost." Keri didn't care so much about the "famous" part. But she embraced the rest of that label. It was her purpose, her mission in life, to try to find those who had gone missing and return them safely to their families.

In her head, she knew that not all of those people could be returned alive, but that was still her goal. And that's why she felt a nagging rawness in her gut, a sense that she had failed Kendra Burlingame, even if the woman was dead before Keri was ever assigned the case. She'd felt this guilt before and she knew that there was only one thing that made it better: time.

It also wouldn't hurt to have distractions and she'd scheduled one for Monday. She was supposed to meet Mags for lunch. When she'd gotten the voicemail message asking if she wanted to meet up, Keri had initially been reluctant. But then she thought about it.

The case was over. There wasn't going to be a trial so there was no professional conflict. And Margaret Merrywether was a hoot. Keri hadn't had a real female friend in years and the idea that Mags might become one filled her with something approaching comfort.

She also suspected that in the wake of Kendra's death, Mags needed a friend right now too. So she was going. She might even let Mags call her Keri instead of "Detective."

As to the rest of her Sunday, after signing off on the case paperwork, it would be off to the hospital to meet Ray, who was being discharged in the afternoon. She planned to give him a ride home—after that coffee, of course—and help square away his apartment so he could function on his own.

As she got up and puttered about, brushing her teeth and getting ready, Keri's thoughts turned, as they almost always did in quiet moments, to Evie.

Standing in the shower at the marina comfort station, also for the last time, she let the warm water lull her into a sort of reverie. She closed her eyes and immediately saw her little girl: blonde pigtails, wide, gap-toothed smile with one chipped tooth up top, eyes as green as emeralds.

If I found her today, would Evie even recognize me? Would she answer to that name anymore? Would she be happy to reconcile or angry at how I failed her?

Keri stepped out of the shower and dried off slowly. Pulling out her phone, she looked at the message from the Collector again.

i was there. you were not. caution is good. you passed that test. but trust is key. maybe next time.

That last line—maybe next time—ate at her. She so wanted to set up a next time right now. Her fingers itched at the thought of typing out a reply.

But she knew she couldn't. She likely only had one more chance to connect with him. If she handled it poorly, he'd be in the wind, perhaps forever.

And right now, she didn't have the ability to pursue him properly. She might have the financial resources, with the boat sale. But all her information was obtained illegally, so she couldn't count on the department's help. In fact, if they learned what she'd done, she could be arrested.

And just as bad, she was pretty sure Jackson Cave was investigating her now. He might be bugging her home. He might be tapping her phone. He was surely having her tailed. And if he got wind of her plan, he might find a way to pass that information along to the authorities, or worse, to tip off the Collector. She had to be very careful from this point forward. She had to behave as if she were constantly under surveillance, constantly being watched.

Because she probably was.

CHAPTER THIRTY EIGHT

Keri, full of jumpy anticipation at the thought of picking up Ray from the hospital, had wrapped up all the case paperwork and was heading out of the bullpen when Hillman poked his head out of his office.

"Locke, I need you in here."

She walked over, trying not to let her nervousness show.

Has he found out about the stakeout at the Promenade? Or worse, the break-in at Cave's office? Has he just been waiting for me to close out this case to fire me?

"Have a seat," he said, motioning to the loveseat.

Noting that he usually directed her to the hard-backed metal chair across from his desk, she reluctantly did as she was told. He sat down in his chair and settled there, unspeaking.

"Yes, sir?" Keri asked, unable to handle the silence.

"Detective Locke," he said, clearly uncomfortable, "I just wanted to tell you that…you should know that…well…good job."

"I'm sorry, sir?"

"I've submitted your name for commendation for your work on this case. When everyone else in the department, myself included, was ready to close up shop, you stuck with it, sometimes in contravention of my direct orders. We'll set that aside for the time being. The point is, this case would not have been solved without your diligence and dedication. I've told Captain Beecher this and she agrees that a commendation is in order. So you know, expect that sometime soon."

Keri forced herself to keep a straight face. It looked like Lieutenant Hillman had been in literal pain as he'd spoken the words. But he had spoken them. And she didn't want to mess up the best interaction they'd ever had with an ill-timed smile.

"Thank you, sir," she said quietly.

"Dismissed," he replied, rediscovering his typical gruff demeanor. But as she reached the door, he added under his breath, "You're welcome."

As she walked out, Keri kept her jaw set, refusing to let anyone see how giddy she felt inside. She hurried through the station, in danger of being late to get Ray, who would tease her mercilessly for it. But just as she got to the outer doors, the desk officer called her back.

"You received a letter yesterday," the woman said.

"Thanks," Keri said, slightly perplexed, and took the envelope. In over a year as a detective she'd never gotten an actual mailed letter. As she walked out to her car, she noticed that there was no return address. She got in and opened it. The note was typed in all caps. It read:

WANT TO HELP. CHECK WAREHOUSE AGAIN. YOU DIDN'T COVER EVERYTHING.

She suspected that this message was from the same raspy-voiced person who'd left her the voicemail telling her to investigate the abandoned warehouse in Palms for information about Evie. That had been a dead end and she would have chalked it up as a cruel prank if not for one thing.

When the techs tried to scrub the call, they couldn't find a thing. The number was untraceable. The voice, while human, had been altered so much that she couldn't even be sure it was male. Whoever had left that message had gone to a lot of trouble to avoid being discovered. Why go through all that just for a prank? It didn't make sense. But with everything that had happened since then, Keri hadn't given it much more thought.

But since the warehouse was on the way to the hospital, and despite her sense that she was being played, she decided to stop by again. It probably wouldn't help but it couldn't hurt.

When she arrived, Keri parked in almost the same spot as last time. She made the short walk to the warehouse, keeping her eyes peeled for anything out of the ordinary, anything she might have missed on her last visit. Nothing jumped out at her.

She walked past the same sign reading *Priceless Item Preservation*, the one that seemed to be taunting her, and entered the warehouse. It didn't look any different than the last time. She did a cursory walk-through of the place before returning to the one unusual spot she'd initially discovered last time.

The metal folding chair still sat above what she knew was a false floor panel, with chunks of drywall resting on the seat. Other bits of drywall debris lay on the floor beside the chair, where they'd fallen when Keri moved it. It didn't look like anyone had been here in the interim.

She slid the chair to the side again and popped the raised button on the wooden floor panel painted to look like concrete. Once again it released easily and she removed it to look at the small hole beneath. There was nothing inside.

Keri sat down on the floor beside the hole and tried not to let her growing frustration get the better of her.

Why would someone do this to me? Just to be cruel? How many wild goose chases am I going to go on before I finally stop putting myself through this?

Keri tried to shake the self-pity out of her head and focus on what was in front of her. Someone skilled had left her that voicemail. Someone had taken the time to follow up with a letter. Maybe there was more to this.

She pulled out the note and reread it:

WANT TO HELP. CHECK WAREHOUSE AGAIN. YOU DIDN'T COVER EVERYTHING.

The first two lines seemed pretty straightforward—purely informational. But the phrasing of the last one seemed a bit off. It was more cryptic. Why not say "you didn't look everywhere"?

Could it be a clue? You didn't cover everything. What does that mean?

Drawing a blank, Keri sighed and grabbed the wooden cover to return it to its place.

The wooden cover—you didn't cover everything.

She stared at the square of wood in her hands for a long second before turning it upside down to look for anything unusual—writing or odd markings of some kind. Nothing.

She shook it. There was the faintest rattle from the inside. She shook the panel more vigorously and again heard the sound. There was definitely something in there.

She felt around the sides, searching for any unusual protrusion. On one side, she found a small indentation, about the size of a dime. She pressed on it hard. There was a tiny click and a thin slot appeared. She turned the panel so that the slot was facing down and shook. One small piece of paper fell out.

Keri put down the panel and picked up the paper. It was a blank piece of plain white paper, about five by seven. She turned it over. On that side was an image, black-and-white, grainy and obviously taken from far away, likely with a telephoto lens.

It was a close-up of a girl, cropped so much that the surroundings couldn't be identified. The girl looked to be about thirteen. Despite being black-and-white, it was clear that she had blonde hair, cut very short. Her face was slack and inexpressive but her eyes were sharp. Her mouth was open slightly and Keri could tell that she had a chipped upper front tooth.

She stared at the image for a long time, unwilling (maybe unable) to draw any conclusions about it. Was it Evie? Was it some Photoshopped image of a random girl meant to torture her? The very fact that she couldn't tell at first glance whether or not this was her daughter made Keri sick to her stomach.

What kind of mother am I that I don't know immediately whether this is legitimate or fake?

She felt the room starting to spin around her, felt the world fading from her control, as it had so many times before. Her breathing became rapid and shallow. The warehouse grew fuzzy. Beads of sweat appeared suddenly on her brow. She felt herself sinking into that familiar panicked despair.

No! I will not let this happen. I will not fall apart. No more. I'm through with this crap. Pull it together, Locke!

And as quickly as the panic attack had started, it was over. Her vision cleared and her breathing slowed. The spinning stopped and the nausea disappeared.

After taking a moment to regroup, she made a decision. She would take the photo to Edgerton to see what he could do with it. She would have the wooden floor panel and the metal chair and everything else in the warehouse searched for prints. She would pursue this lead with the same ferocity that she followed every lead involving Evie.

But she would no longer allow herself to be the victim, forever at the mercy of her loss and the moments of uncontrollable terror it caused. She had to stay strong for Evie and, just as important, for herself. For one way or the other, she would find her daughter.

Evie, hang on, she called out to her silently. *I'm coming for you.*

A TRACE OF VICE
(A Keri Locke Mystery—Book 3)

"A dynamic story line that grips from the first chapter and doesn't let go."
--Midwest Book Review, Diane Donovan (regarding Once Gone)

From #1 bestselling mystery author Blake Pierce comes a new masterpiece of psychological suspense.

In A TRACE OF VICE (Book #3 in the Keri Locke mystery series), Keri Locke, Missing Persons Detective in the Homicide division of the LAPD, follows a fresh lead for her abducted daughter. It leads to a violent confrontation with The Collector—which, in turn, offers more clues that may, after all this time, reunite her with her daughter.

Yet at the same time, Keri is assigned a new case, one with a frantic ticking clock. A teenage girl has gone missing in Los Angeles, a girl from a good family was who duped into drugs and abducted into a sex trafficking ring. Keri is hot on her trail—but the trail is moving fast, with the girl being constantly moved and with her abductors' single, nefarious goal: to cross her over the border with Mexico.

In an epic, breathtaking, cat and mouse chase that takes them through the seedy underworld of trafficking, Keri and Ray will be pushed to their limits to save the girl—and her own daughter—before it is all too late.

A dark psychological thriller with heart-pounding suspense, A TRACE OF VICE is book #3 in a riveting new series—and a beloved new character—that will leave you turning pages late into the night.

"A masterpiece of thriller and mystery! The author did a magnificent job developing characters with a psychological side that is so well described that we feel inside their minds, follow their fears and cheer for their success. The plot is very intelligent and will keep you entertained throughout the book. Full of twists, this book will keep you awake until the turn of the last page."

--Books and Movie Reviews, Roberto Mattos (re Once Gone)

Book #4 in the Keri Locke series will be available soon.

BOOKS BY BLAKE PIERCE

RILEY PAIGE MYSTERY SERIES
ONCE GONE (Book #1)
ONCE TAKEN (Book #2)
ONCE CRAVED (Book #3)
ONCE LURED (Book #4)
ONCE HUNTED (Book #5)
ONCE PINED (Book #6)
ONCE FORSAKEN (Book #7)
ONCE COLD (Book #8)

MACKENZIE WHITE MYSTERY SERIES
BEFORE HE KILLS (Book #1)
BEFORE HE SEES (Book #2)
BEFORE HE COVETS (Book #3)
BEFORE HE TAKES (Book #4)
BEFORE HE NEEDS (Book #5)

AVERY BLACK MYSTERY SERIES
CAUSE TO KILL (Book #1)
CAUSE TO RUN (Book #2)
CAUSE TO HIDE (Book #3)
CAUSE TO FEAR (Book #4)

KERI LOCKE MYSTERY SERIES
A TRACE OF DEATH (Book #1)
A TRACE OF MURDER (Book #2)
A TRACE OF VICE (Book #3)

Blake Pierce

Blake Pierce is author of the bestselling RILEY PAGE mystery series, which includes seven books (and counting). Blake Pierce is also the author of the MACKENZIE WHITE mystery series, comprising five books (and counting); of the AVERY BLACK mystery series, comprising four books (and counting); and of the new KERI LOCKE mystery series.

An avid reader and lifelong fan of the mystery and thriller genres, Blake loves to hear from you, so please feel free to visit www.blakepierceauthor.com to learn more and stay in touch.

CPSIA information can be obtained
at www.ICGtesting.com
Printed in the USA
LVOW13s0128300317
528931LV00012BA/209/P